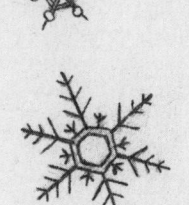

Praise for

JUST BEYOND THE
VERY, VERY FAR NORTH

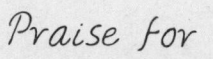

"A return to the Very, Very Far North is a welcome thing, indeed, and readers who fell in love with Duane the polar bear and his company of friends will welcome them back with open arms."

—*Booklist*

"Readers are reunited with Duane the Polar Bear and his cast of vividly imagined friends. . . . For fans of gentle animal stories or those looking for examples of how to navigate interpersonal challenges."

—*School Library Journal*

JUST
BEYOND
the
VERY, VERY
FAR
NORTH

JUST BEYOND the VERY, VERY FAR NORTH

a further story for gentle readers and listeners

By Dan Bar-el

Illustrations by Kelly Pousette

ATHENEUM BOOKS FOR YOUNG READERS

New York   London   Toronto   Sydney   New Delhi

ATHENEUM BOOKS FOR YOUNG READERS
An imprint of Simon & Schuster Children's Publishing Division
1230 Avenue of the Americas, New York, New York 10020

Interior design by Karyn Lee
The text for this book was set in Mrs Eaves OT.
The illustrations for this book were rendered in charcoal and digital.
Manufactured in the United States of America
0821 MTN
First Atheneum Books for Young Readers paperback edition October 2021
2 4 6 8 10 9 7 5 3 1
The Library of Congress has cataloged the hardcover edition as follows:
Names: Bar-el, Dan, author. | Pousette, Kelly, illustrator.
Title: Just beyond the very, very far north / Dan Bar-el; illustrations by Kelly Pousette.
Description: First edition. | New York City: Atheneum Books for Young Readers, [2020] | Audience: Ages 8–12. | Audience: Grades 4–6. | Summary: Duane the polar bear and the other animals of the Very, Very Far North find their friendships deepening as they are challenged by the arrival of a contentious weasel and an unexpected departure.
Identifiers: LCCN 2019043788 | ISBN 9781534433441 (hardcover) | ISBN 9781534433458 (pbk) | ISBN 9781534433465 (eBook)
Subjects: CYAC: Polar bear—Fiction. | Bears—Fiction. | Animals—Arctic regions—Fiction. | Friendship—Fiction. | Arctic regions—Fiction. | Humorous stories.
Classification: LCC PZ7.B250315 Jus 2020 | DDC [Fic]—dc23
LC record available at https://lccn.loc.gov/2019043788

For anyone who has ever done something kind for someone else,
just because
—D. B.

For my dad, who always stressed the importance of adventure,
especially with good friends
—K. P.

THE INTRODUCTION

I F YOU HEAD NORTH, true north, to the truly north part of north, where icebergs shiver, where thermometers lose confidence, and where snowflakes prefer to avoid, and then once you reach *that* north, you go just a little bit further north, that's where you'll find Duane the polar bear and his friends.

It is a world apart, but it's familiar all the same.

Should Duane, upon meeting you, offer a Snow Delight, do not hesitate in accepting, as they really are quite delicious. And while you're slurping away, if C.C. suddenly asks you where you've come from, it's not because she is nosy; she is simply gathering scientific data. Should you feel a tickling at your left ear, followed by a tickling at your right elbow, turn around as quick as you can and you may just catch Magic before she scampers off, giggling. If Handsome pays a visit, a hasty hair combing is highly recommended. Should Major Puff drop by, it's best to avoid all gull-related conversation, and if Twitch has accompanied him, then prepare yourself for yet more nibbles and possibly some cardio-hopping afterward. And should you notice a quiet creature grazing nearby, well, that's just Boo's way of saying hello.

Some of you may have already visited Duane, as I understand that he snuck in a personal invitation at the end of the previous book. But for those of you who have limited time, due to banjo lessons or croquet practice, or because your parents really do need looking after, then this second story I'm about to tell will tide you over until you are ready.

1.
DUANE AWAKES, FINDS HIMSELF AMONG FRIENDS, AND THEN FINDS SOMEONE LESS FRIENDLY

ONE DELIGHTFULLY BITTER, COLD morning, Duane woke up from a long, long, *very* long nap. He stretched what needed stretching. He scratched what needed scratching. He yawned for a full minute and a half. With the claws of his front paw, he brushed his white polar bear fur until he felt that he looked presentable. Then he ventured out of his cave.

"Hello, Duane," said the half dozen individuals

already gathered. "We've been waiting for you."

Duane smiled sleepily. The bright sunshine caused his eyes to narrow, but even still, he could see that everyone who mattered to him was there.

"Hello, C.C.," he said to his friend, a snowy owl.

"What's up, Magic?" he asked his friend, an arctic fox.

"Morning, Major Puff," he said while saluting his friend, a puffin.

"Lovely to see you, Twitch," he said to his friend, an arctic hare.

"Salutations, Handsome," he said to his friend, a musk ox.

"Hi, Boo," he whispered to his skittish friend, a caribou.

Certain that no one had been left out, Duane opened his big, powerful arms as wide as they could spread. "Group hug, everyone!" he declared. And then he pulled all his friends in close, except for C.C., who flew up in the air because, as she's always maintained, she is *not* a touchy-feely kind of owl.

"So what did I miss?" Duane asked.

"What did you miss?" said Magic incredulously. "What did you *miss*? What *didn't* you miss, would be the easier question, Duane." Magic has a tendency to overexcite. The others shuffled their feet or groomed themselves absentmindedly until her point was made and conversation could continue. "You've slept through most of the winter. There have been blizzards and iceberg breakings and strange creature sightings and at least a billion other things. I mean, *really*!"

Duane nodded apologetically, which is Magic's favorite response. Then he said, "In that case, let's begin with what I didn't miss, since the list would surely be smaller."

"You didn't miss the comet, which, according to my calculations, will be flying above us in two weeks. Two weeks!" squealed C.C. with a shudder of delight before gaining control of herself.

"Fortunately for you, you haven't missed my gripping solo reenactment of the Great Puffin War of Eighteen-Something-Or-Other," declared Major Puff proudly. "Will there be marching, you ask? Oh, yes, there will be plenty of marching!" At which Major Puff proceeded to demonstrate by marching around the group with feet raised high.

"And you didn't miss my upcoming birthday, thank goodness," said Handsome, "because etiquette would then require that I give you cold harsh glares of disappointment. Such expressions never look good on me, and all that face-tightening just adds wrinkles."

"You didn't miss my first attempt at public singing," whispered Boo.

"What was that?" asked Duane, but Boo just shook her head self-consciously and hid behind Handsome.

Before any plans for the day could be suggested by his friends, a breeze carried the sweet smell of wild berries up to Duane's nose, which he inhaled to his great delight. His stomach, now stirred and fully awake, wasted no time in growling a plan of action that Duane obediently relayed to the others. "I think a post-nap snack is what's necessary. We could all visit the berry bushes on the way to the Fabulous Beach for a picnic."

Duane's friends know there is no point in arguing with Duane's stomach, and there are worse things to do than spend a day at the beach in one another's company. With little fuss, they made their way down the hillside toward the ocean's edge.

"Might we stop briefly at my abode so I can take

along my brush?" asked Handsome. "I find the salt air tangles my hair, leaving it a matted mess."

"Ooh, and if we pop by me and the Major's place," said Twitch, "I'll bring along some meringue cookies I whipped up this morning. And some carrot cake and a selection of tarts."

"Then that's what we shall do," agreed Duane.

"But Duane," moaned Magic, while flopping on the ground and sighing very dramatically, "then we will never get there!"

"We will. I'm absolutely sure of it." He gave Magic a smile for encouragement. "Major Puff, would you do us the honor?"

"Understood," said the puffin, who rushed toward the front of the group. "Follow me, lads! Left, right, left, right, and so on!"

Duane lingered back, allowing everyone to proceed before him. He took a moment to acknowledge his fortunate circumstances. To think that he'd come to the Very, Very Far North from somewhere else and was able to make himself a home that was cozy, and friends who meant the world to him. Duane sighed, and without a doubt, it was a happy sigh. The day was proving itself to be a very pleasant one, requiring little effort on Duane's part to keep it so. In a short while, he would be eating sweet nibbles and warming his belly under a springtime sun.

But just as he was about to join his friends, a most disagreeable rush of noise overwhelmed him. Clanging and booming and bonging and rumbling, the cacophony was so loud and violent, it shook the ground beneath his paws.

Oh my, thought Duane.

Was it an earthquake? An avalanche? These were questions best left for a less chaotic interlude. At that moment, Duane could only manage to reach up and cover his ears as the din continued to assault him from all sides. He wanted to run away and find safety, but he couldn't. His legs were wobbly, unresponsive; they wouldn't move forward no matter how much he willed them to. Duane was terrified.

Meanwhile, his friends *were* moving farther

and farther away. Soon they would be gone, out of sight and out of hearing range. Oddly enough, they seemed unaffected by the deafening noise. Could they not hear it? Why was it not throwing them off-balance like it was doing to him? These, too, were questions best left for later. Right now, Duane needed their help. He yelled for them to come back, or at least he tried to, because while his legs might have been unsteady, his voice was just plain stuck. It made no sense. His jaw was wide open, his intentions were urgent, yet nothing came out of his mouth but a silent scream.

Now, before you get too swept up in the unsettling, even scary situation I've just described, I will take this moment to tell you that nothing in this story so far is real. Duane hadn't really greeted his friends or planned a picnic or suddenly found himself helplessly in the grasp of an overpowering ruckus. That is because Duane was still in his cozy cave, lying on his soft mattress, having a terrible, terrible nightmare. I apologize.

I should have been more forthcoming about this fact. It's just that in my opinion, no story is ever improved by telling a reader that it has all been a dream. Yet in this case, it's unavoidable. Duane was asleep, albeit fitfully, and even if his nightmare scream was soundless, his real scream—the one that finally woke him up—was very, very loud, as you will soon learn.

"AH!"

Duane sat up in an instant. His face was flushed, and his body was trembling. Those of you who have had bad dreams may recognize Duane's confusion as he took in his surroundings, found his bearings, and realized that he was no longer in the dream but back in his cave, alone.

"Oh my," he whispered aloud.

But although he was awake, the noise had not ceased.

Bong! Clang! Clang! Bong! Clang!

The source of Duane's nightmare was apparently coming from the grandfather clock tucked in the corner. *How unexpected*, thought Duane. For as long as he had had the old timepiece, it had offered nothing in the way of conversation but a steady, calm, and reasonably quiet *tick-tock*. Now, for some unexplained reason, it had decided to add pealing and tolling to the mix, and was doing such, I should add, with reckless abandon.

Clang! Dong! Bong! Bong!

This was most strange. The grandfather clock no longer had hands on its face to tell general time, and therefore had forgone its duty to announce any specific time. Since relocating the clock from the Shipwreck many, many months ago, Duane felt he had come to understand the language of *tick-talking*, so from his point of view, the clock must surely be upset about something important and needed to make it abundantly clear.

"There, there," Duane said to it gently as he walked over. "What seems to be the problem?"

To his surprise, and to yours, too, I should imagine, the grandfather clock spoke back. Amid all the clangs and bongs, an angry voice from within yelled, "Where is it?"

Duane took this in stride. He figured that if he was able to understand clock language, it stood to reason that given enough time, the clock would learn to speak his. "Where is what?" Duane asked.

Bong! Clang! Clang! "Argh! Come on, where did it go?"

Duane leaned in closer. "Perhaps if you describe what you're looking for, I can help you."

"Arrrgh!" growled the clock, seemingly ignoring Duane's generous offer.

But *was* it the clock speaking? Now that Duane was closer, he could hear other sounds besides the clanging and the yelling. He could hear scurrying and scraping as well. Intrigued, Duane used his claws to pry open the long, thin panel on the clock's belly. What he saw inside the grandfather clock, among the weights and chains, the pendulum and other metal doodads noisily flying about, was a small, furry creature who appeared to be in the middle of a big, furious tantrum.

2.
A MOST UNPLEASANT ENCOUNTER

WHEN I LAST LEFT off, Duane had come face to face with an uninvited visitor who was causing noise and havoc inside the grandfather clock Duane kept in the corner of his cave. Did I mention it was a Monday? It was a Monday. All stories involving overly loud characters begin on a Monday.

"Arrgh! Gum-dollop-puckered-bibble-sputtin-malapropy thing! Where are you?"

Said creature was tubular in shape, with short, stubby legs and a thin tail half the size of his body.

Wiry black whiskers framed his snout, his ears were small and round, and his eyes were black and beady, and not in a good way. What I have just described is known commonly as a stoat or an ermine, or what I will now refer to as a weasel. The fact that he would distinguish himself further by saying he was a short-tailed weasel, when his tail is obviously fairly long, only begins to demonstrate just how badly this creature knows himself. In any case, whatever he was, Duane had never laid eyes on one before.

"What are *you* looking at?" the weasel demanded as soon as he realized he'd been discovered.

"I suppose I am looking at you," replied Duane honestly.

"Well, cut it out! Mind your own business! And shut the door!"

Obediently, and delicately, Duane did so.

Bong! Clang! "Argh!" *Clang!* The clamor within the clock continued as Duane stood beside it, taking in what had just happened. Despite the rude awakening and the rude behavior he had just encountered, he did not respond in anger. I think it is fair to say that Duane was not prone to those darker and sometimes crueler feelings. Instinctually, he would not assume someone else to harbor those feelings either, so he was always willing to give them the benefit of the doubt. *Perhaps it is just his way of expressing himself,* Duane thought. Then he pried open the grandfather clock's front panel once more.

"You again?" growled the weasel. "What part of 'shut the door' didn't you understand?"

"None of it," replied Duane sincerely. "I understood all three words. But I do have two questions. Will this search of yours be going on for much longer? And second, is there a name that you go by? My name is Duane. If you don't have a name, I am very good at giving them. In fact, all my—"

"If there is any name-calling to be done, I'll be the one doing it, *Duane!*" interrupted the weasel. And he said Duane's name with such contempt, it was as if he were spitting out some foul-tasting medicine. "But to answer your questions: One, when I'm finished! Two, None of your business! Now, *shut* the door!"

Obediently, and delicately, Duane did so again.

Clearly, this was not how Duane expected his day to start out. And technically, it was now daytime. From outside the mouth of his cave, dawn was breaking. An intense sunbeam cut through the bruised purple clouds, made a beeline into Duane's home, and bathed him in golden light. As if taking his cue from the sun, it suddenly dawned on Duane that the visitor might simply be grumpy because he hadn't had breakfast. Duane's stomach often behaved the same way when it was empty. Ready to extend an invitation, he pried open the grandfather clock's front panel a third time.

"Argh!" shouted the weasel after getting hit straight-on with a blinding spotlight of sunshine. "That's it! I'm outta here!" The weasel jumped off of the grandfather clock and pushed Duane aside, or at least tried unsuccessfully to push him—there was a substantial size difference between the two.

"Before you go," said Duane, "I wanted to ask you if—"

"More questions?" screamed the weasel. "You really are a few flakes short of a blizzard, aren't you?"

Duane wasn't sure what the visitor meant by that, but his instincts were now strongly suggesting that whatever it meant was probably not very nice. Duane also reconsidered if a breakfast invitation was such a good idea after all. He chose a different question instead. "I'm sorry to bother you, but I have to ask—have you lived in the clock all the time I've had it?"

This question amused the weasel. His anger subsided, or rather, he replaced it with a tone that was snide. First he laughed in a most unpleasant way, with all the joy and lightness squeezed out of it. "Oh, is that what you think, *Duane*?" He then moved right up to Duane and stood on his hind legs, with his thin little chest puffed out. "You think I spend my days holed up in this silly contraption? Is that what you think, *Duaney-Duane* (*poke, poke*)?"

Duane gasped. The visitor had addressed him just like Magic sometimes did, complete with the poke to his belly, albeit this time to his knee, on account of, again, the weasel being so much smaller. But whenever Magic poked him, Duane knew it was done playfully. When the weasel did it, he felt mistreated. Uncomfortable feelings bubbled up inside the gentle polar bear that he'd never experienced before.

For my part, I'm sorry to add that the weasel will be making more appearances in the book from time to time. However, on the plus side, he will be leaving this scene shortly, but not before spreading more of his . . . well, whatever the opposite of charm is.

"It's all la-di-da with you, isn't it, *Duane*? I bet you think you have a happy, wonderful life."

Duane couldn't disagree. He'd felt quite fortunate that he'd found the Very, Very Far North and all the friends he'd made since. Just thinking about it made him feel blissful enough to sigh contentedly.

But seeing that satisfied smile on Duane's face made the weasel angry again. *His* face grew flushed. "Well, too bad for you, because it ain't gonna last! It ain't how the world works!"

"What do you mean?" asked Duane, genuinely concerned. "How does the world work?"

With Duane hanging on to his words with rapt attention, the weasel's personality warmed slightly, because he now had the kind of spotlight he really desired. "Well, Duane, let me tell you a story. Imagine the ocean ice in the springtime," he began confidently. "One moment you're strolling on it together with your friends, nothing but sunshine and giggles. But then cracks start to form, and the ice begins to break, and the next thing you know, you're all on your separate floes, floating farther and farther apart. That's how the world works."

"But couldn't I just swim over to my friends?" asked Duane.

"Ha! You think they want you on their little ice

raft, taking up precious space and eating half their food?"

"Oh, wait, do we have food in this story? In that case, I would plan ahead and bring more food along with me to share before the ice cracked."

"No! That's not the point!" the visitor shouted.

"Or I could bring along rope, like the kind I saw on the Shipwreck. We could all hold on to it so that our ice floes don't drift too far apart. We would stick together and figure things out."

"No! Stop it!"

"Or better yet, before we even step on the ice, we ask C.C., who is very clever, to examine it for safety."

"No, no, no!" screamed the visitor in a petulant rage. "Sheesh! The point is that everyone gets along until they don't get along, okay? End of story."

The visitor stomped away in a snit, leaving Duane wondering if he'd ever heard a less satisfying ending to a tale. As far as understanding how the world works, he honestly felt less enlightened than he was a minute earlier. As for the weasel, Duane didn't know what to think. On one hand, he felt sorry for the visitor, who seemed always angry and frustrated and suspicious. *That can't be pleasant for him*, Duane thought. On the other hand, being in the visitor's company seemed to churn up some of those same feelings in him.

The weasel was still searching through Duane's home, darting here and there. He burrowed under Duane's mattress and rummaged through the drawers of his dresser, and all the while, he cursed and spat and screamed, spinning a dark cloud of discontent out of the air around him. When he finally gave up the hunt, he turned on Duane aggressively. "You!" he shouted.

"Me?" asked Duane cautiously.

"Yeah. There's a large dried crumb in this dump somewhere. I was pretty sure I stashed it in the clock, but it ain't there. It's mine, got it?"

Silently and slowly, Duane nodded his comprehension. *That was what all the fuss was about?* he wondered. *Just for a crumb?*

The weasel gave
the polar bear one
final sneer, as a
way of farewell,
I suppose, and
then scurried
out of the cave
and quickly out of
sight.

"And to think he
might have enjoyed a whole
bowl of breakfast berries with me," Duane mused
aloud. "Oh well."

With his home quiet again, Duane could catch
his breath. And thinking of berries reminded
Duane that he might as well have his breakfast,
because the morning was quite present and ready
to take the day forward. The polar bear filled a
bowl with berries he'd picked the day before, and
was sitting at his table about to dig in when he was

interrupted by loud stomping and yet more yelling.

"Have you gone daft, Duane? Did you awake last night with the sudden urge to recreate the sound of an orchestra tuning up?"

It was Handsome. He was looking none too happy. He did, however, look as if he managed to brush his hair before angrily storming up to the cave, which may account for his delay in arriving.

"I'm sorry, Handsome," said Duane.

"Sorry doesn't cut it! Your nocturnal mayhem jolted me from my slumber and left me turbulent and aghast! May I remind you that one needs a proper amount of restful sleep or one's face will cultivate unsightly puffiness. I cannot afford to look ridiculous!"

Being not fully awake, Handsome had overlooked removing the white wrinkle cream around his eyes. It made Handsome appear as if he were in a never-ending state of shock. Duane felt it best not to mention it.

"You are absolutely right, Handsome. I didn't mean to be rude. It's just that I had a horrible nightmare."

"Oh . . . Oh, I see," replied Handsome, the blustering, angry wind in his sails now subsided. "Then I apologize for my outburst."

"But as you are here, and we are both awake, would you care to join me for breakfast?"

Handsome agreed to the invitation, even though there was next to no advance warning, and the two friends gathered at the table to break bread—or chew berry, as the case may be. Duane considered telling Handsome about the visitor and what the visitor said about how the world works, but he hesitated. It was information he needed to digest on his own, when the unpleasant, churned-up feelings in his stomach settled. So instead, he let Handsome go on about his evening grooming rituals and the ten most important rules for avoiding bags under one's eyes. Duane was still distracted. He could only nod and smile in response. He was perhaps going through the motions, as one says. But at least they were the motions of friendship, and that would do for now.

3.
C.C. VISITS THE BURROW, TWITCH OVERDOES IT, AND MAJOR PUFF IS GIVEN A SCARE

DURING THE FALL SEASON, Twitch invited C.C. over to the burrow for an informal get-together with her and Major Puff. For C.C., this was a new experience, and one she might normally have declined, as it did not advance scientific knowledge in the least. More importantly, an informal get-together would involve chitchat. Chitchat baffled C.C. She'd be the first to admit it.

What possible value can be gained from talking about trivial subjects? she wrote in her Personal Journal of Scientific Inquiry, which is like a diary, but much, much more serious. *I have observed that chitchat jumps from one unimportant topic to another, with no goal in mind. It is, scientifically speaking, a waste of breath.*

It is perhaps worth pausing to note how differently some of C.C.'s friends approached the act of chitchatting. Major Puff saw it as an opportunity to bring up one or twelve stories of his brave ancestors battling their dastardly foe, the great black-backed gulls. Magic saw it as a way to insert unbelievable, made-up facts into the conversation. Then, when someone challenged or laughed at them, as someone almost always did, it allowed her to fall on the ground dramatically and sigh heavily until the awkwardness of it all made everyone apologize. But more than anyone, Handsome excelled at chitchatting. He understood that chitchat was the oil that greased the steering wheels of friendships. C.C. would likely point out that friendships, unlike real ships, do not require wheels to steer. Handsome would beg to differ, explaining that friendships are always moving, and if you wish to guide them away from a rocky, hazardous shore of misunderstanding, make sure your friendship is lubricated with enough chitchat to turn on a dime. And if Duane had been listening to this discussion, he would have asked if the subject was still chitchat or if it had moved on to sailing.

I have observed, C.C. continued, writing in her Personal Journal of Scientific Inquiry, *that my life with friendships has been overall more interesting than without them. Therefore, I conclude that an afternoon of chitchat is the required "grease" to keep them in working order.*

With her conclusion reached, and her acceptance of Twitch's invitation given, C.C. set herself to the task of researching subject matter that could serve useful for chitchat. Inversely to her dislike of chitchat, C.C. adored research, so in that regard, anyway, it wasn't all useless.

Meanwhile, back at the burrow, Twitch's thoughts were less about the chitchat and more about the nibbles. As you may well know, any informal get-together typically includes refreshments such as tea and cake, or tea and pie, or tea and cookies. An informal get-together hosted by Twitch typically includes tea along with cake, pie, *and* cookies, in several different varieties, as well. I'm sure we would all agree that by any estimation, that is a ridiculous amount of nibbles to have on offer for a small group of three. The reason for this is complicated.

In matters of food, it is said that for some, "their eyes are bigger than their stomach." It is the difference between the amount they *think* they want to eat, and the much lesser amount they actually can handle. With Twitch, one might say it was an issue of her *heart* being bigger than her *friends'* stomachs. She took great pleasure in seeing expressions of joy on everyone's faces as they bit into a favorite nibble that she had personally baked. But the thought of someone being disappointed because the nibble on offer wasn't what they wanted caused Twitch distress in equal measure. Unfairly, she felt it a failure on her part not to have anticipated their preferences, and to avoid that feeling, she put in much, much more work in pleasing her friends than she perhaps needed to.

So, the day before the informal get-together with C.C., Twitch sat down in the communal area of the burrow and planned her menu. A problem quickly became evident. Duane and her other friends always expressed their preferences about nibbles in some obvious way. Twitch had taken note of who grabbed what nibble first or who went for seconds or what nibble caused someone to involuntarily say "Mmmm." But C.C. wasn't so expressive in such matters. It occurred to Twitch that she didn't really know what C.C. liked. The arctic hare took a deep breath and didn't panic.

"Must have cake," she said to herself. "Cake is required. Few can refuse a slice of chocolate cake. Or sponge. Or honey. Or Bundt. Especially Bundt! Better make the Bundt. And the other three as well."

Within seconds, Twitch committed to baking not one but four cakes.

"Ooh, but what if C.C. is a cake-hater? Or an icing-avoider? Not likely, but still a chance, a possibility. The world is big, it takes all kinds, just saying. Best to have a pie on hand too. Can't go wrong with apple. Or cherry. Or apple-cherry. That's settled, then! Make all three. And a rhubarb."

For those of you keeping score, that's now four cakes and four pies.

"Yes, a lot of work ahead of me, without a doubt. But that's the way the cookie crumbles, so best get on with it. Oooh, cookies! Forgot about them! You can't deny that there are those who prefer *les petits bonheurs*, excuse my French."

"Did you say something, Madame?" asked Major Puff, who had just entered the communal area.

"Hmm? Oh, the topic was cookies, Major. Not so hard to make, not difficult. A bit of batter, roll into balls, pop in the oven, just saying. Why not make two varieties of cookies if they're a snap to make? Oooh, gingersnaps! There's a tasty type. You like those, don't you, Major? Gingersnaps?"

Major Puff wasn't really paying attention as he was now fully engaged in his morning marching practice. "Left, right, left, right, stiff back, Major! Get those webbed toes higher! Left, right, left, right, that's more like it! Sorry, what was that, Madame?"

Twitch also wasn't paying attention as she was now fully engaged in naming cookie varieties. At the same time, her back feet began thumping at a faster and faster pace. "Arrowroot, biscotti, custard cream, hardtack, Florentine, macaroon, and short-bread, chocolate cream, chocolate chip, chocolate dip, chocolate chunk." By the time she proclaimed the formidable-sounding "chocolate chunky chip dipped in cream cookie," Twitch had launched herself off her chair and into the kitchen, grabbing an apron and a mixing bowl mid-flight.

"I don't know what kind of cookie C.C. likes!" she screamed, very much in a panic.

For the rest of the day and beyond, through morning until evening, through free time and through bedtime, through the next day's breakfast time and lunchtime and even through her gentle stretching and cardio-hopping time, Twitch baked and baked and baked. By the time C.C. arrived at the burrow and tapped her beak against the door at exactly three o'clock, the burrow looked less like a home and much, much more like a bake shop. There were square cakes, round cakes, either double-layered or triple-layered. Some were jam-filled, while others were icing-covered. There were cream pies and fruit pies, of apple, banana, lemon, berry, rhubarb, and combinations thereof, all laid out in alphabetical order. As for cookies, it would be easier to state what variety of cookie was *not* on offer: raisin. There were no raisin cookies. Of every other kind of cookie, there were plenty.

Tap, tap, tap, tap, tap.

"Hello, C.C.," said Twitch, opening the door.

"Hello, Twitch," replied C.C. back, and then

added, "Your burrow is pleasant and adequately suitable for habitation." This was too soon a compliment to pay to her host, being that C.C. hadn't actually entered the burrow yet. C.C. was perhaps a tad eager to delve into the chitchat using the list of talking points she'd researched and had been practicing.

"How nice of you to say. Won't you come in, dear," said Twitch with a welcoming gesture.

After thirty-one uninterrupted hours of baking, Twitch radiated a calm and relaxed energy. Her smile was serene. Had C.C. studied Twitch's face, she might have gone so far as to say that Twitch looked sleepy or exhausted, but C.C.'s attention was drawn to the cloud of flour that filled the air when Twitch's front paw ushered her inside.

C.C. scanned the common room of the burrow in search of Major Puff, the reason being that the greater part of her prepared chitchat comments were devoted to the subject of migration. It was, after all, approaching the time of year when the

Major left on his own migration—that was in no way a vacation, I should stress. C.C. thought her timing was apt. Her research produced a whole range of migration-related facts and observations that she was sure would grease her relationship with the puffin.

But Major Puff was nowhere to be seen or heard. What she did observe were three chairs off to the side facing one another in an isosceles-triangular configuration. *This is likely where the serious chitchat will commence*, C.C. noted to herself. Then she took in, with far less interest, the large, rectangular table completely overwhelmed and straining under the weight of nibbles. C.C. wasn't particularly curious about the absurd number of pastries until it dawned on her that among it all was Major Puff. Allow me to explain.

You see, earlier in the day, Major Puff saw the mountain of sweets as an opportunity to hone his camouflage skills. A military strategist of Major Puff's caliber never discounts the element of surprise. It may be precisely that advantage that makes the difference in battling with his long-time foe, the great black-backed gull, whenever that should be. So just before C.C. arrived, he hopped on the table and stealthily blended in, mainly with the vanilla and chocolate cakes, but for the exception of his orange beak. For that, he thrust his head out just enough to put it in front of the carrot cake.

"Hello, Major Puff," said C.C. "I didn't see you at first."

"As was expected," said the puffin with a smirk of satisfaction. Then he jumped off the table and

led the snowy owl toward the set of chairs.

But before C.C. could actually sit, Twitch, whose eyelids were drooping considerably, came over and joined them. "Won't you have a nibble," she offered, gesturing toward the table with a sweep of her arm, releasing another cloud of flour into the air.

Dutifully, C.C. walked over and studied the nibble-laden table intensely for a solid minute. She scanned the staggering number of scrumptious pies and the monstrously huge, elaborate cakes before deciding upon a single plain arrowroot cookie that she took back to her chair. Twitch was about to encourage C.C. to take some more—to take, in fact, a *lot* more—but a big yawn forced its way out instead.

C.C., meanwhile, dived straight into the chit-chat. "*You* should be much fatter," she said to Major Puff. As you might imagine, the statement threw him off-balance.

"Oh? Oh! But—uh, wh-wh-why exactly?" the puffin finally asked.

"In preparation for your upcoming migration. The exertion on your body will be very strenuous. You will lose many calories every day, which is why you need to add weight now before you leave."

"I-I do?"

"Yes. If you don't, you might wither away until you are just feather and bones."

"Oh my, that would be awful," acknowledged the puffin, absentmindedly rubbing his belly with a wing.

"Speaking of adding weight," interjected Twitch, "could I interest you in another nibble, C.—*yawn*—C.?"

Showing good manners, and despite barely finishing what she had already taken, C.C. again approached the table overburdened with fancy cakes and tantalizing pies, and again chose a single plain arrowroot cookie. A distressed squeak escaped Twitch's lips, which then induced in her a yawn so powerful, she nearly fell off her chair. The yawn also caused another puff of flour to expel from her, which lingered in the air, giving Twitch a somewhat hazy appearance.

"I trust your aquatic skills are up to standard," said C.C., quickly turning back to Major Puff and continuing on with her next topic of chitchat.

"Er, my . . . m-m-my what?"

"Aquatic skills. Swimming and treading water or floating," C.C. explained. "As you've probably already experienced during past migrations, a powerful ocean storm might appear suddenly. Storms have the potential to force birds such as yourself into the water, where drowning is certainly an option."

Major Puff had indeed experienced a storm during one of his migrations. In fact, it took place on his first migration. It was awful and terrifying and he had purposely blocked out the memory, vowing never to think about it again and never ever to migrate on days in which the weather was even excessively breezy, never mind stormy. He'd kept that promise to himself for all these years, until C.C. reminded him of it.

"Oh, the sheer horror," he whispered, the memories flooding back. Major Puff grew very quiet, his eyes took on a blank stare, and his face grew as pale as Twitch's face, now that the flour dust had settled on her.

"Speaking of—*yawn*—drowning," said Twitch very slowly, with eyes all but closed, "could I—*yawn*—interest you in some—*yawn*—saltwater taffy cake?"

Neither Major Puff's trauma nor Twitch's exhaustion made any impression on C.C., who, on the contrary, was judging that the informal get-together was going quite well. She seemed to be excelling at the chitchat. This, in turn, relaxed her and whetted her appetite.

"I will pass on the cake, but I will indulge in another arrowroot cookie. They are more than the sum of their nutritional values," C.C. replied, attempting a lavish compliment for her host, which Twitch may or may not have heard. Twitch's chin had since slumped forward onto her chest, and she was barely moving.

Unfazed, C.C. stood and walked over to the dessert table with a bounce in her step. She happily snatched her third cookie and returned to her seat. This time, when she turned her attention back to Major Puff, he flinched involuntarily as his eyes met C.C.'s with a pleading look of fear.

"Major Puff," began C.C., causing the puffin to scrunch his eyes shut in trepidation of the next round of chitchat. "Will you keep a journal?"

"Enough, I beg you!—Sorry, what?"

"Will you take notes of everything you observe on your migration so that you can share them with Twitch upon your return?"

Major Puff didn't answer right away. He took a moment to compose himself, finding that his feathers were damp with perspiration for some reason. Perhaps an overcommitment to his noon-time marching practice would account for it? He wasn't sure. "A journal, you ask? It's, um, it's not the puffin way. We hold to an oral tradition. I will share my heroic tales with Madame, no doubt."

At that moment, Twitch let out a big, loud snort, which drew both of their attention. A bit of mumbling followed, mostly inaudible other than the last part that sounded like "I need a nibble holiday, just saying." Afterward, Twitch fell into an even rhythm of gentle snores. She was fast asleep.

This was not lost on C.C. "I see that I have overstayed my welcome," she said to Major Puff. "Thank you for a lovely afternoon. Please pass on my appreciation to Twitch when she awakes."

Major Puff walked C.C. to the door. He clicked the heels of his webbed feet together and then gave her a respectful bow as a way of saying goodbye. C.C. left thinking about the expression "time flies when one is having fun." She made a mental note to develop some kind of experiment that could test that theory scientifically.

After closing the door behind C.C., Major Puff turned toward the table filled with a mountain of untouched sweet delights. He wondered how much flying would be required to reduce him to nothing but feather and bones. He imagined what he might look like, withered, shrunken, wasted. It caused him to shudder. Instead of waking up Twitch, to inform her that the get-together had now concluded, he decided to let her be. While she slept and snored, he began filling a plate full of cake chunks and pie slices and stacks of cookies. He gorged himself from that afternoon up until the late evening, until he could barely walk for the heaviness of his belly. If he was to begin a migration right then and there, it might require a lot of effort to get him off the ground and into the air. But if he did manage flight, he was sure to have plenty of calories to burn before he'd be in danger.

At around midnight Twitch awoke. Major Puff had gone to bed long ago, so she had no one to help her put together the day's events. There were gaps in her memory. She did remember C.C. arriving, and she did remember vaguely a disappointment about all her baking being unappreciated. But that couldn't be true. When Twitch turned toward the table of desserts, she found a sizable amount of nibbles consumed. It looked as if a hungry horde had attacked it, so she must have misremembered. C.C. apparently loved all her baking. Still tired, Twitch shuffle-hopped down one of the burrow tunnels to her own bed, comforted by the thought that her efforts hadn't gone to waste.

4.
MAJOR PUFF'S MIGRATION AND THE SEND-OFF THAT DIDN'T HAPPEN

C.C.'S IDEA OF CHITCHAT was enough to turn Major Puff off casual get-togethers forever. And as for migrations, which were not a holiday in the slightest way, the whole idea of one was now tainted with overwhelming worry. How different it was hearing C.C.'s facts about deadly storms and starvation compared to back when he first met Twitch, who spoke in reverent tones about his migrations. Then, the puffin had felt the rush of heroic blood through his veins, and he was looking forward to making the next journey if only to describe it to Twitch later upon his return. Now, not so much.

To be fair, Major Puff had brought this attention upon himself. He'd felt less and less threatened by a sudden attack from a great black-backed gull, enough so that he started shifting from his usual topic of conversation—historical puffin battles against said enemy—to recounting his harrowing personal experiences of flying south. "And there I was, terribly off course," he regaled his listeners on one occasion, "no clue as to my whereabouts, when suddenly I found myself surrounded by a squadron of Canada geese! Good lads, all and all, very polite—almost too polite—but the constant honking left me stunned."

What resulted from this shift in storytelling was that as the season changed, it was not him but his friends who would be the first to turn the conversation to his migration. In fact, the very next week, Handsome had said, more or less, the same thing, albeit not before making it first about himself. "As winter approaches, I once more find it harder to see my reflection in the pond. The days and nights cool, and the surface begins to freeze. A horrible sign of things to come, but I suppose you welcome it as a harbinger of your upcoming journey."

The week after that, when Major Puff left the burrow and headed toward the meadow where he performed his high-intensity marching workouts, he found that Magic had put up arrow signs. They were scattered everywhere. Some signs said SOUTH and others said MIGRATION THIS WAY, but all the signs were unhelpfully pointing in different directions.

It seems even Boo got in on the discussion. "You should just tell her you like her," she said in her usual quiet voice. In all honesty, Major Puff didn't really hear what she said, but he suspected it had to do with migration.

Inevitably, the question everyone asked was

when exactly he intended to leave. Major Puff would hem and haw, make vague predictions, and try to change the subject. It wasn't until Twitch decided to have a send-off party for him that Major Puff was forced to set a definitive date for his departure. There. The deal was done. Signed and sealed, as the expression goes. Everyone promised to show up and wave goodbye.

The night prior to liftoff was fraught with anxiety for the poor puffin. The fact was that more than any other time in his life, Major Puff was content with where he was. The burrow was cozy and warm, and leaving it, along with everything and everybody in it, didn't appeal to the Major as much as it once did. It's very possible that he might have conceded this point, swallowed his pride, and announced to all his friends that he no longer wished to go. But during that long, dark night of soul-searching, Major Puff was visited by the weasel.

It was as if this creature could smell the hesitation in the air, as if all the Major's fears of danger, and his concerns for not looking cowardly, were tasty morsels to be ferreted out and gorged upon, and in doing so, the weasel made a bad situation worse.

"What kind of friends throw a party to celebrate your likely end?" said the weasel by way of announcing himself.

Major Puff fell backward as he squawked in surprise. "Eeek! Who's there?" Fortunately, his room was at the far end of a tunnel a fair distance away from Twitch's, so she was not disturbed. When the puffin's eyes adjusted to the dark, enough to turn the ominous silhouette before him into the slightly less ominous appearance of the weasel, Major Puff was able to calm himself enough to ask two questions. "Um . . . I'm sorry, but what was that you said?" followed by "And, um . . . have we met before?"

The weasel ignored both and continued on his train of thought. "I'm just pointing out that here you are, about to go on a very dangerous trip where you will most likely die."

"W-w-will I?" Major Puff's face looked pained. "To the best of my knowledge, I haven't so far."

"Just increases the odds of it happening this time," insisted the weasel. "But instead of talking you out of it, your so-called friends decide to make it a whoop-de-do. Doesn't seem right, if you ask me."

Major Puff's fear turned to confusion. It never occurred to him that his friends' interest in his perilous journey might not be sincere. "When you put it that way, uh . . . no, I suppose not."

Unbeknownst to the Major, the weasel was enjoying himself immensely. Hidden by the darkness was a grin as wide as it was twisted. "Of course it's not right! And let me ask you this, Major Puff, sir . . . who else would want to be celebrating your tragic misfortune, hmm?"

There it was. Like a strike of a match, or perhaps a cast of a spell, those were the words that formed the idea that turned the puffin's confusion into mistrust. "W-w-why, the great black-backed— do you mean to say that—"

"What do I know?" replied the weasel with fake humility. "I'm just connecting the dots, that's all. Safe trip, Major. It was nice knowing ya." In the snap of a tail, he was gone.

Major Puff stood squeezed in the corner of his dark room for quite some time, lost in thought, unsure of what to feel. Had he read his friends so poorly? Had he not seen their trickery? The sleepless night dragged on and on.

The next day, when the time arrived for his departure, everyone came around the burrow to see Major Puff off, but he was nowhere to be found. Twitch hopped outside. She was agitated. "Not in his room. Not getting in one last practice march along one of the tunnels. Isn't like him to leave all stealthily if not under attack, or at least thinking he was under attack."

"Perhaps we mixed up the time and day," suggested Duane.

"Which is why I insist on proper invitations!" jumped in Handsome, with a great deal of passion. "To all gathered here, please take note of the chaos such confusion creates. Civilized life hangs by a delicate thread. Invitations, proper napkins, good diction—I'll say no more."

Magic would have none of it. "Even if we did get it wrong, why would he leave without saying goodbye? I mean, really! Twitch is obviously hurt by it, and she probably baked a lot of nibbles for the occasion, right, Twitch?"

"Hmm?" Twitch was indeed concerned about Major Puff and not really paying attention. She spoke absentmindedly, in a flat voice. "Yes, plenty of nibbles, sweet and savory, I do hope the Major is all right, so strange, and tea, there's tea, too, why wouldn't he wait to say goodbye?"

"Exactly! Plenty of nibbles!" declared Magic, completely missing the more important issue at hand. "So we should help Twitch out and probably eat them so they won't go to waste, right, Twitch?"

"Hmm? Yes, the nibbles, shouldn't go to waste, made the Major his favorite, gingersnaps, he likes those, thought he'd be pleased, have a good parting memory, just saying." In a daze, Twitch slowly went back into the burrow to fetch the food.

A heavy silence hung over the assembled friends. Major Puff's surprise departure was a mystery. "He didn't even want to go," said Boo.

But no one heard her, and then almost at the exact same time, C.C. announced loudly, out of the blue, "I recently discovered I like arrowroot cookies." The puzzled expressions on her friends' faces in response informed C.C. that she hadn't yet mastered the art of chitchat, and another heavy silence followed.

The happy send-off that was supposed to demonstrate everyone's affection for Major Puff ended up being a very somber affair. Nibbles were eaten, but not with much enthusiasm. Duane observed it all with a sense of confusion and sadness. If it were just a case of miscommunication, a wrong time given or a wrong time heard, then the results of such a small error seemed way out of proportion. *Maybe it isn't just civilized life that hangs by a thread*, Duane thought. *Maybe friendship too is as fragile and susceptible to an ill breeze.*

5.
DUANE MAKES AN UNEXPECTED
DISCOVERY IN A CAVE NOT HIS OWN

NOT TOO MANY DAYS after, as the temperature dropped lower and lower, the first snowfalls arrived in the Very, Very Far North. The light dusting of white upon the landscape brought out a particular beauty that bewitched Duane like no other season did. An adventure hike was in order, without a doubt, so he left his cave to take in the sights.

Duane could have gone in any direction. Why he chose to head toward the river, and then to cross it, could not be explained as anything more than a whim on his part. But why Duane chose to hike farther still, beyond his usual territory, weaving his way between mountains he'd never explored before, speaks to an understanding of the world that defies rational explanation. As your narrator, I suggest to you that perhaps there are other threads that involve themselves in our daily affairs, connecting us. Invisible as these threads may be, they still hum with energy if, like Duane, we are sensitive to their pulse. How else to explain why the polar bear found himself approaching a cave? A cave quite similar to the one he calls his home, but this cave was currently in the possession of Major Puff.

Before the puffin was seen by Duane, he was first heard. "Left, right, left, right, come on, Major, get your feet up higher and keep your mind off dinner!" The voice was unmistakable. But why was it coming from down here, in this isolated location, when it should be speaking from up there, in the sky, southbound en route to a much warmer place? "Dastardly unpleasant, cruel and unusual, so cold and empty, not fair, I say. Could be in my cozy burrow but for those traitors leading me on," the voice continued mumbling. "Snap out of it, Major! You're a Puff! Don't let the Puff name be sullied with self-pity. Keep marching! Left, right, left, right, that's more like it."

Duane reached the cave's mouth, stood to one side, and cautiously peered in. He gasped. Major Puff did not look good. Aside from the clearly sub-par marching, his feathers were matted, his wings were drooping, his body was undernourished, his haggard face suggested a puffin lacking in sleep— but it was Major Puff's eyes that frightened Duane the most. They kept shifting in expression from terror to hurt to anger to suspicion. The thread that connected the concerned polar bear to the poor, disheveled puffin tugged at Duane's heart.

Duane stepped forward and made himself known. "Major Puff?" he said gently.

The puffin immediately threw himself into an

aggressive stance, which for a puffin with military prowess means stepping back defensively. "Who goes there?" he demanded.

"Me. Your friend Duane."

Despite the warm smile that accompanied Duane's introduction, Major Puff would have none of it. *"Pah!"* he spat. "I have no friends."

The rebuke stung. But as Duane was convinced that Major Puff was not well, he chose to ignore the comment and instead stepped a bit closer. "Why are you here, all alone in this cave? Shouldn't you be on your migration?"

The question infuriated the Major. "Oh, you'd like that, wouldn't you? I'm sure all of my so-called friends would like me flying off on my migration, eh?" The puffin demonstrated his defiance by assertively stepping back again.

Duane was confused, not least of all because of a puffin's tactic of running away whenever he was showing force. What Major Puff was saying confused Duane even more. "Why, yes, of course we would like that." He took another step deeper into the cave and closer to the Major. *Thump!* Duane banged his head against the cave's ceiling, which apparently was not as high as at the opening. To compensate, he crouched lower and tried to ignore the sharp pain as he spoke on. "Shouldn't we support you, if it makes you happy?"

Major Puff was of two minds. On face value, Duane's answer was both caring and encouraging, but likely this was yet another cunning trick. He stepped back again. "These trips—which are *not* vacations—are very dangerous! They can be fatal! Is this your idea of support? Letting me go forth on such a mission?"

Duane could not understand why Major Puff was so agitated. He wanted to calm his friend. Still crouching, he stepped closer. *Thump!* Again, he banged his head against the hard, rocky ceiling of the cave, which apparently continued to taper lower and narrower the farther he ventured in. This time, Duane went down on his four legs. "Major

Puff, I believe that I speak for all your friends when I say—*ow* . . ."

"Ow?" asked Major Puff.

"No, sorry, not ow," Duane explained, rubbing his sore head. "What I meant was . . . we would say that we'd prefer if you *didn't* go on your migrations that are not in the least holidays. We know they are dangerous. We've always known that, and it would sadden us if you were to get hurt. But we also know that it's your choice to make, not ours."

Major Puff stepped back, this time not out of anger, but because he was overwhelmed by Duane's explanation, which in his heart he knew was true and sincere. In doing so, he found himself up against the back end of the cave, which he leaned on to steady his cold, tired body. "You really mean that?"

"Of course," replied Duane.

"I don't know what got into me. I was led to believe that you were all colluding with the great black-backed gulls."

Duane, still upon all fours, with a head that was throbbing, wasn't sure he'd heard right. "Wait, who would tell you such a thing?"

"Some small, unpleasant creature. I did not know him, but he seemed to know me all too well. I daresay he was convincing enough for me to leave the burrow angrily before any of you arrived for my send-off."

Duane had his suspicions of who that unpleasant creature might be, but even so, it still didn't explain everything. "But why are you hiding away in this cold—and I will now add, very cramped—cave, Major Puff?"

The puffin stared at Duane in great distress. He tried to fight through it, stood up straight, and declared, "I don't know!" Then just as quickly, his wings drooped down again, his head bent, and he spoke through tears long held in. "I didn't want to fly south. I enjoy the burrow. It's cozy and warm and I believe that I am well-liked, which is a new and pleasant experience, and . . . and . . . to be quite honest, I find that migrations are very taxing on the nerves."

Major Puff let out a huge sigh. The burden of his secret was cast off. He felt lighter but also embarrassed by his confession. Duane, however, felt nothing but sympathy and admiration for him, as well as an unrelated headache. When their eyes met, he gave Major Puff a small nod of understanding. A moment of silence passed in which the puffin regained his composure. Without any bluster, he said to Duane, "I would appreciate it if you would be so kind as to keep this between ourselves."

Balancing himself on just three legs, Duane leaned forward to extend to the puffin his paw in friendship. "I give you my word, Major Puff, that nothing will leave this cave." *Thump!* *"Ow!"* The third whack to his head dropped Duane onto his belly with his snout beside the puffin.

You would be forgiven for thinking that the natural conclusion to this story is that Duane and Major Puff would leave the very cramped cave together and return to their respective homes. It certainly was what Duane and Major Puff were thinking. In fact, Major Puff said exactly that. "At this point, I think the proper thing to do is inform Twitch that I shall be remaining through the winter."

Duane, with his belly still flat upon the cave floor, and believing he'd received his fair share of thumps for the year, smiled feebly and said, "Agreed."

Then nothing happened.

And then nothing continued to happen.

Major Puff cleared his throat. *"Ahem.* Problem, Duane?"

"I'm not sure," said the polar bear.

"You're not sure?" asked the Major.

Duane scrunched up his face and grunted as if he were trying to do a very difficult task. When he eventually stopped, he said, "I'm sure now. There *is* a problem. I'm stuck."

"You're stuck?" confirmed the Major, for the sake of clarity.

"Completely stuck," Duane clarified further. "It really is a very cramped cave."

"Indeed," replied the puffin, who was standing between a rock face and a polar bear's snout. "Suggestions?"

Duane's head hurt . . . a lot. Bits of the cramped cave were wedged uncomfortably into his waistline. Dare I say that in his immobile condition, his derrière was left exposed to the open side of the cold cave. Taken in total, the whole affair was tiring Duane out. "I think it's a wait-and-see situation, Major."

"Oh, how so?"

"I need to lose a little weight in order to thin myself enough to back up. So I suggest . . .

YAWN! . . . I *suggest* . . . a long nap for all. *Mmmm-ah-phu-zzzzzz-snort.*"

And that was that for the polar bear. Like Twitch after a marathon baking spree, Duane was out cold. Major Puff applied a few gentle pokes to Duane's snout, but it was clear that he was beyond reawakening and there was little the puffin could do to remedy it. So Major Puff took stock of his situation. Yes, the cave was considerably smaller than before. On the positive side, there was still air circulation, and with Duane now blocking most of the entrance, the cave was also insulated and warm. "Well, Major," he said to himself, "we are under siege, as it were. Pinned down with nowhere to go. As a brave puffin warrior, our options have been reduced to one." And so, Major Puff squatted down beside Duane and promptly joined him in an extended nap.

Three days later, Duane awoke feeling much, much better and slightly thinner, enough so that he could push backward and free himself from the cave's grip. Major Puff took a leadership role and barked orders and encouragement during it all. "That's right, lad! Keep wiggling! Don't give up! Stiff upper lip, loose hips, and so on!"

The fresh winter air that greeted them outside was cold and invigorating. They both gave a shake to loosen the accumulated cobwebs in their heads, after which Duane's stomach wasted no time in getting his attention to point out that there were at least ten to twenty meals unaccounted for. Duane began walking back home, assuming that Major Puff was of the same mind. When he glanced to his side, he discovered it was not so. The puffin had not followed in his direction.

Duane turned. "Are you not going back to your burrow?" he asked.

Major Puff was still in the process of deciding. Unlike Duane, he did not sleep right through the previous days. At several points he awoke and had time to ponder things. He knew now that he didn't have to migrate if he didn't wish to, and he acknowledged to himself truthfully that he found migrations quite frightening. What didn't sit well with him was the idea that his fears were in control of his life. The puffin didn't want to *not* do something only because he was afraid of it. He was a Puff. He had standards to uphold.

"Major?" asked Duane again, but this time in a tone of playful suspicion. "Are you thinking of going on your migration after all?"

Major Puff gave Duane a confident smile, filled with youth and vigor. "Maybe once more for the thrill of it," he replied with a wink. "See you in the spring, lad!" And with that, the puffin launched himself into the sky and flew away.

Despite his stomach complaining impatiently, Duane watched his friend fly higher and higher until he disappeared among the clouds. Duane silently wished him a safe journey, admiring the puffin's courage and his self-pride. There was no doubt that he would honor Major Puff's wishes and not tell anyone about their encounter. He would allow the Major to explain about what had happened the day of his departure when he was ready to do so, after he returned.

6.
DUANE SHARES A BEAUTIFUL SNOWFALL WITH HANDSOME AND C.C.

IT WAS A WINTER morning, still early in the season, in which Duane awoke to a snowfall like no other he'd ever seen. The day was windless. The flakes fell from the sky, large and leisurely, taking all the time in the world to float down and join their cousins below. Together they knitted an ever-thickening blanket, tucking in the Very, Very Far North for the frigid months ahead. Duane, who was no longer tucked in, or asleep or even sleepy, stood at the threshold of his cozy cave, staring out in silent contemplation, hypnotized by the graceful snowflake performance.

It's as if they are all dancing, he thought tenderly.

Eventually, though, his serenity was overtaken by his curiosity, as was often the case. So, without a second thought, without a plan or a destination, Duane made his way outside and followed where his curiosity led. However, he did stop briefly to snap off a long icicle hanging at the cave's mouth, to lick and slurp while he explored. He'd been saving *that* particular icicle for just such an occasion.

Duane trundled down the mountainside, which soon led him past Handsome's field. To his surprise and delight, there was the musk ox, also awake and standing in the middle of his clearing, just as mesmerized by the snowflakes as Duane had been earlier. He was looking up at the blue-gray, cloud-washed sky and smiling brightly. Duane thought Handsome appeared younger. Gone were the worry lines, the harsh creases that could mark his face whenever he gazed into the reflective pond during the unfrozen days or into his hand mirror during the others, because even while admiring his own beauty, Handsome would still be scrutinizing himself for blemishes and flaws.

But there was none of that this morning. Handsome was under the snowfall's disruptive spell, happy and carefree. He stuck his tongue out and waited for a flake to land. When one did, he swallowed it delicately, savoring it like a fruit sorbet or a tart at an afternoon tea. Then he stuck his tongue out again. Two flakes landed this time. Handsome giggled. Turning his head to try another location, he caught sight of Duane, icicle in hand, staring back at him from within the shimmering white curtain of falling snow. I will tell you truthfully that Handsome did not blush in embarrassment, nor did he attempt to overcompensate with a stern expression to show he was above scrutiny. No, he just continued smiling, meeting Duane's gaze with the same giddy joyfulness. He sauntered over to

Duane, who had resumed his icicle slurping. Seconds passed in mutual silence, and then, as if the circumstances made it clearly obvious what should happen next, they took off together to explore this winter dream, side by side.

Traveling west, they reached the open lands. Flat and uneventful was how Duane would usually describe this area. His least interesting exploring happened here unless something bad came along, like a blizzard. But on this snowy morning, the ground was as smooth and blank as a painter's canvas, an unquestionable invitation for creative expression. The polar bear and the musk ox separated, step by step, farther and farther away, a line of hoofprints heading diagonally in one direction, a line of paw prints heading diagonally in the other. And then Handsome turned, so Duane turned too. Their tracks curved inward. Put together, it looked like an incomplete heart. As Duane and Handsome came closer, they shared a laugh but did not stop advancing. Their snow prints crisscrossed, each now continuing in the opposite direction, but soon again curving and returning, then crisscrossing and leaving, over and over in tighter and tighter weaves until they braided themselves into a pair of friends together once more.

When they turned around to observe their drawing, the heavy snowfall had all but erased it. There would be no record of this moment. It was fleeting and had passed. But they were not disappointed, because they too were living from one moment to the next. They went at it again, this time separately.

Handsome clomped out a giant outline of the hand mirror that Duane had once given him as a present. Duane tramped out a giant bowl of berries he wished to eat come spring. "Ah!" said Duane, and "Ho, ho!" said Handsome, in recognition of each other's pictures.

"Do what I do, Handsome," Duane said.

Handsome watched as Duane created a large half circle. At the top of it, Duane curved his steps away into a smaller half circle to the side, and then twisted the line again until it pointed upward. Handsome copied Duane's drawing. When combined, the musk ox knew exactly what they drew. "That's my head! Those are my horns!" he declared ecstatically. "Now it's my turn!"

Duane studied Handsome tracking out a very large oval into the snow. Once completed, Handsome delicately sidestepped to the right and marked out an identical oval. Then, demonstrating more musk ox agility than Duane would have thought possible, Handsome jumped into the middle of the oval, stomped a large dot, jumped sideways into the first oval, did exactly the same, and finally leaped out and away, leaving his finished picture for Duane to guess.

"Wait, I know this. It's . . . it's . . ."

"Yes, Duane?" Handsome encouraged.

"Those are C.C.'s eyes!"

"You are correct, sir," said Handsome, most pleased.

For Duane, thinking of C.C. while holding his now half-finished icicle pop brought up the fond memory of another winter get-together. It had taken place at the Fabulous Beach. It had involved him and C.C. and the invention of the delicious Snow Delight. *The company of one friend had been lovely and tasty*, he thought, and thus he now figured that adding a second friend to the mix could only double the pleasure.

"How would you feel about a stroll to the shore of the Mainly Frozen Ocean next?" Duane casually asked Handsome, knowing that his friend was not always keen on exploration and might say no.

Happily, however, the idea was well received. As noted, Handsome was possessed of a free, untroubled spirit that morning, so he had no reservations about heading there too.

Off they went.

The snow continued to fall steadily, abundantly and silently. Lost in his thoughts, Duane considered how much wiser it was for the clouds to release their snowflakes one by one, rather than dumping them all out in one go. Such an event would be frightening if you weren't prepared for it. The sudden loud thump, the heavy weight, it would seem as if the sky had broken off and fallen. *Fallen off of where?* he then wondered. *What is the sky attached to? What if after it breaks off, it leaves a big hole up there? What would you see through the hole?* Duane smiled to himself. He was sure that these were all excellent questions to ask C.C., who always appreciated a challenge.

At the Fabulous Beach, Duane peered out in the distance, toward the Shipwreck. By late morning, the relentless snow had softened its hard, dark outline, making it difficult to discern. Optimistically, Duane was hoping that C.C. would see them on the shore. If it had been a bright day, the sun might have caught a glint off her telescope, letting him know that she was watching. However, on this day, with the cloud layer so thick, the sun could barely manage even basic lighting, settling instead for a meager translucent glow. Duane gave the Shipwreck a big, sweeping wave of his arms just in case.

"Who are you waving at, Duane the polar bear?"

Once again, to Duane's delight and surprise, and most definitely against all probability, there was C.C. perched nearby him. The snowy owl was living up to her description because a large pile of snow had accumulated on her head, resembling a too-large hat and indirectly suggesting that C.C. had been standing there, in one place, for some time.

"I was waving at you," Duane explained. "I thought you might be on the Shipwreck conducting experiments for the advancement of knowledge toward the benefit of all. But now I can see you are here." Duane paused, mouth open, suddenly acknowledging the "against all probability" element I had just mentioned. "Why *are* you here, C.C.?"

"I was waiting for you, Duane the polar bear."

"You knew that we were coming here?"

"No, I saw that you were coming here," C.C. explained, "while I was *outside* conducting experiments for the advancement of knowledge toward the benefit of all. I have six weather stations to check on, located in different areas that I visit. Each one measures atmospheric pressure, humidity, wind speed, air and ocean temperature, and precipitation. Once I gather the information, I apply formulae in order to make reasonable predictions."

"So you saw us coming here?" said Duane, repeating the only part of C.C.'s explanation that he understood.

"Yes, while I was flying above."

Meanwhile, Handsome, who'd been standing there the whole time semi-listening, was looking very, very bored. He sighed loudly to make his feelings known.

"It wasn't difficult to see you," C.C. continued, "having such very, very big eyes as I do." C.C. said this last part while looking directly at Handsome. She said it as she says all things, in a matter-of-fact voice, without much emotion, but Duane wondered if she had seen Handsome's snow drawing of her from the sky and was expressing her hurt by the depiction.

Either way, Handsome was oblivious to it all. The snow was falling, he was happy, and the conversation, in his opinion, had gotten dull. "I wish to recite a poem that I've just composed in my head," he announced. "I feel that the occasion calls for it."

Duane smiled approvingly, and both he and C.C. gave Handsome their attention.

"*Ahem* . . . Oh, gentle snowflakes, soft as musk ox fur, each one an orb of beauty, on that we all concur."

"Good job," said Duane. "I could hear the rhyming words."

"I don't concur," said C.C. "Snowflakes are not soft like fur; they are ice crystals. They are also not round in the slightest."

Handsome was annoyed. "I'm not finished yet. Allow me to complete my poem *before* you pounce on it with your criticism."

"I was liking it," Duane threw in meekly.

"Ahem!" Handsome cleared his throat much more forcibly. "Oh, *spiky* snowflake, with six to fourteen spokes—"

"Always six," C.C. interrupted.

"SO unexpected your arrival, that greeted us when we awoke."

"Not for me," countered C.C. "I calculated a heavy snowfall several days ago."

"AHEM!" yelled Handsome, forgoing any actual throat-clearing. "Oh, *likely* snowflake, bereft of color, starkly white—"

"White is not the absence of color. From a physics point of view, one might say that white is actually all colors combined. When we consider wavelengths—"

"Enough!" shouted Handsome, his nostrils flaring.

Duane cringed in his discomfort. He knew that C.C. couldn't help but point out errors when she heard them, but he also knew with certainty that Handsome's feelings *were* hurt. This was not going to go well.

"The problem with you, C.C.," said Handsome in a voice dripping with disdain, "is that you have no romantic soul. You see only facts and figures, whereas I, and everyone else, see beauty and all that is sublime! Poetry is wasted on you."

C.C. stared back at Handsome for what felt to Duane like an eternity. He grew more and more fidgety. His plan to double the pleasure among friends was clearly in need of rethinking. Should it have been obvious to Duane that Handsome and C.C. were too different in who they were to share this experience? Was he supposed to keep his friendships separate? Duane felt guilty. He was reminded of his encounter with the weasel and his story about things not lasting, friendships not holding together. Was he responsible for Handsome's current state and now C.C. having her feelings hurt? *Were* her feelings hurt? Duane found it hard to tell with C.C. what she was feeling. He had good reason. C.C. herself had a hard time figuring out what she was feeling.

In that silence, C.C. was weighing Handsome's words. Being a very clever snowy owl, even by the standard of other snowy owls, she understood *what* Handsome was saying. All things considered, she would have to agree with him. For her, facts and figures *were* important. But it was *how* he'd said it that she was grappling with. C.C. recognized the anger in Handsome's face, but the tone of his voice was new. Objectively, it sounded as if Handsome thought less of her, as if she were not just different from him, but actually lacking something important in her character that made her broken. *Was* she incapable of seeing beauty in the world?

The silence proved unbearable for Duane. He needed to step in right away. He opened his mouth, prepared to come to C.C.'s aid. He was too late.

"It's not true," C.C. spoke suddenly, looking straight and confidently at Handsome. "You are wrong. I see beauty and understand poetry. And I can prove it too."

With a show of great conviction, C.C. pushed off into the snow-laden air and flew away. Two blinks of a musk ox and a polar bear later, she returned. "I should have mentioned to come meet me at the Shipwreck."

7.
C.C. MAKES HER POINT

C.C. LEFT A SECOND time, flying toward the blurry figure of the Shipwreck, surrounded and gripped by ice. Although Duane had either swam or walked to C.C.'s home countless times, Handsome had never made the journey. For one thing, C.C. had never extended a formal invitation, which was no trifling matter for Handsome. For another thing, swimming was always a big no-no grooming-wise for the musk ox, and walking across the Mainly Frozen Ocean in the winter suggested peril.

"Will the ice support me?" he asked Duane.

"I suppose so," Duane replied. "You're not much larger than I am. I could go first, and you could follow, up until any point that the ice cracks beneath me and I fall in the water, in which case you should probably stop following."

"Agreed," said Handsome.

It didn't go unnoticed by Duane that Handsome accepted C.C.'s challenge without argument, despite his fear of risk-taking. Duane pointed this out.

"It's true. A slip on the ice will not be amusing, nor will a sudden plunge into ice water be invigorating in a good way. But I directed some harsh words toward C.C.," Handsome explained. "My anger was sincere, but my mind is not closed. I would like to see this proof of hers. Shall we?"

So Duane led his noble friend Handsome across the ocean ice, slowly and unsteadily, with a few precarious missteps, but without any painful mishaps. Ever closer they edged and slid and shimmied toward the Shipwreck, where C.C. was awaiting them. They entered through the gash in the Shipwreck's bow, then climbed several sets of stairs midway within the boat until they were again outside, on the upper deck.

C.C. was already there, at the back of the ship, in the location ridiculously named the poop deck. Please contain your giggles if you haven't already done so. The word comes from the original French word *poupe*, which means stern. My goodness, how does any story involving an old ship get beyond that silly detail, I ask you? To continue, there was C.C., and beside her was a contraption almost as tall as her, made mostly of brass. It sat on a stand and was long and skinny for the most part, with little knobs at the side, and beside it was a stack of small rectangular pieces of glass. As I really do not wish to do any more describing of the object, let me just cut to the chase and say it was a microscope, of which you probably know, but Handsome and Duane did not.

"This is a microscope," said C.C. right away, thus catching everyone up to speed. "It is a tool of science whose function is to offer hidden insight of the world. It does not try to prove beauty or explain poetry."

Handsome scrunched his face in an expression of confusion mixed with annoyance. Surely, he hadn't risked life and limb on the precarious ice only to be shown the exact opposite of what was promised back onshore. "I'm afraid you've lost me," he said to C.C.

The snowy owl was not done. "Duane the polar bear, I would like you to take one of these slides," she said, pointing to the stack of glass, "and catch

one snowflake upon it. Handsome the musk ox, you stand here, beside the microscope."

Duane was thrilled to have something to occupy himself with. It reduced his nervous tension considerably. And as tasks go, it was not too difficult. With the snow never ceasing to fall from the sky, simply by extending the glass slide out in front of him he managed to land a flake in very little time. "I've caught one!" he shouted.

"Good. Please bring it to me."

Duane did as he was told. C.C. had him place the slide on a flat part of the microscope called the stage. Suspended straight down above the slide with the snowflake was a tube that contained a lens. It quite resembled a much smaller version of the telescope that C.C. had placed at the front of the ship, to see things that are far away. However, with her microscope, something entirely different was going on. C.C. looked into the top end of the tube, then adjusted a knob to one side, using her beak. She looked again, followed by the adjusting of a second knob. This continued on for longer still until Handsome grew utterly bored.

"Is there any purpose to all this knob twiddling? My delicate fur is developing an icy veneer as I stand here waiting. What is the point?"

"This is the point," said C.C., inviting him over.

Handsome leaned his head down so that one eye peered through the top end of the microscope. As he did so, C.C. explained. "What you are looking at is a snowflake magnified three thousand times. As you will notice, it is neither round nor soft."

"Oh my," gasped Handsome.

"What do you see?" asked Duane with anxious curiosity.

It was difficult for Handsome to speak. What he was witnessing left him literally breathless. "It's . . . It's so beautiful. So delicate and . . . and perfect."

C.C. wanted to reiterate that a single snow-flake such as the one that Handsome was observing is actually a snow crystal, because a snowflake could mean a bunch of crystals that met in midair and clustered together. But she didn't point it out because she suspected it wasn't information that falls under the beauty category.

"I see six branches," Handsome continued, "all growing from a single point. And each branch has tendrils jutting out along its stem, and each tip holds a six-sided saucer. It is a work of art! It is the poetry at the very heart of life!"

C.C. wanted to point out that crystals refer to any material made of atoms or molecules lined up in a regular pattern. She wanted to explain that the kind of ice crystal Handsome was looking at would be classified as a *dendritic crystal with plates at ends*. But she didn't point any of that out because she suspected it wasn't the kind of poetic information Handsome could appreciate.

"Always six, never more," she actually did say aloud, because, well, even snowy owls can get their feathers ruffled from time to time when facts go loosey-goosey.

Eventually, after much pleading, Handsome

relented and allowed Duane to have a look through the microscope too. Again, there was much oohing and aahing. Once C.C. proposed they look at more samples, the excitement grew even bigger because they soon realized that no two snow crystals were exactly alike.

"Did you see how that last one had needles pointing upward, Handsome?"

"Oh, indeed, Duane. Unlike the previous one, so much simpler, but in perfect harmony."

"I'll go catch another! Get ready, C.C.!"

All the while, the snow continued to fall, or dance, as Duane had put it, never in a rush and always with more on the way. The morning hours stretched well into the afternoon, with Duane scrambling eagerly to trap another falling crystal, C.C. adjusting her instrument to bring it into focus, and Handsome swooning at what he observed while choosing the right poetic words to frame it in. At no point did he stop to apologize to C.C. for what he'd said earlier, and at no point did C.C. feel that she wanted an apology. At no point either did Duane stop to give a sigh of relief and acknowledge how things turned out for the better. Because when three friends are so invested in an activity, in the goodwill and laughter it brings, in the warmth of a shared experience that has enveloped the three of them, there is no time to stop. Maybe it is because on these occasions it seems as if time itself has stopped, or as Duane's armless grandfather clock would tell you, there simply *is* no time.

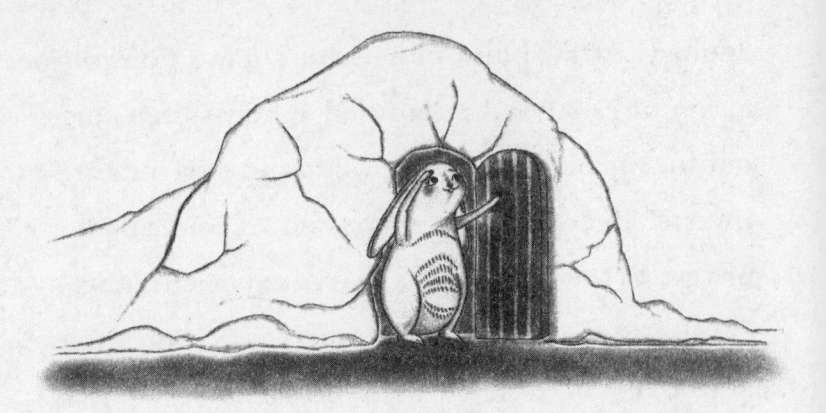

8.
SNOWBEAR

THE HEAVY SNOWFALL THAT transfixed Duane and Handsome at the start of winter turned out to be the first of many in the Very, Very Far North. Over days and more days, the blanket of snow grew ever thicker. Beautiful as it may have been, the novelty wore off for some. The higher the snow level rose, the more of an inconvenience it proved to be. Handsome found it "irksome and exasperating, as are all things done to excess," as he put it. Trudging through the thigh-high accumulation within his field dampened Handsome's mood and gave him the most uncomfortable feeling along his underbelly. But for the smaller friends, Twitch and Magic, the snowfalls were literally overwhelming. Their burrow and den got lost under the buildup; their freedom was hampered.

On the day that this story begins, Duane decided that he would help out his friends by performing some snow removal. It was a Saturday, you understand. All stories involving snow removal begin on Saturdays.

For those of you readers and listeners who have experienced snowy winters where you live, it goes without saying that when it comes to snow removal, the number one tool of choice is the shovel. Sadly, Duane was not in possession of a shovel, nor was there one to be found upon the Shipwreck. But as the snow was sticky, Duane discovered an ingenious alternative. At the mouth of his cave, he gathered up enough snow to form a ball. Then he put it on the ground and began to roll it away from his cave and down the hill, along the path he usually took. The snowball grew larger the farther he pushed, while at the same time, a snowless passageway was left in his wake.

Continuing down the hill, he eventually passed between the two long hills where Magic made her home of tunnels. Duane now began rocking the ball of snow sideways, both left and right, up each hill's slope, and in doing so, uncovered the many entrances of Magic's den. Each time another hole was revealed, Magic's head would instantly pop out with a word of appreciation.

"Thank you, Duane!"

"You're welcome, Magic."

"Thanks a bundle, Duane!"

"No problem, Magic."

"Thanks a million, Duane!"

"It was my pleasure."

"Thanks-a-rooney, Duane!" "Thank you-a-rama!" "Thanka-thanka-thanka, Duane!"

"Okay, okay, okay," he giggled back.

After all den entrances were cleared, and all expressions of gratitude depleted, Duane continued along the path, farther down the hill, until he sidled up to Handsome's field.

"Good day, Handsome," said Duane.

Not too cheerfully, the musk ox looked up from his hand mirror. "Who is your rotund companion, Duane?" he asked, referring to the ball of snow that was now as tall as Duane but also wider.

Duane looked around him confused. "Um . . . there is no companion."

"Yes, yes, I was making a joke," Handsome explained in a dour tone.

"Ah, I understand," Duane said, although he didn't really.

Handsome sighed sadly. "Apologies. I'm afraid that my sense of humor may have frozen along with my belly in this cold deluge of dandruff."

"You mean the snow?" asked Duane, making sure he wasn't misunderstanding again.

"Yes, I mean the snow," Handsome confirmed.

"Well, in that case, I think I can help you out. But first, I will continue pushing this—Oh! My companion! I get it now!—down to the Fabulous Beach, and then I will return."

This was easier said than done. If the "companion" was Duane-sized at Handsome's field, it was inching its way to being Shipwreck-sized the closer he pushed it toward the Mainly Frozen Ocean. Duane grunted and groaned in his exertions. Whatever you may have heard about how difficult it was for King Sisyphus to push a boulder up a mountain, I assure you it was just as hard for a kind, helpful polar bear to push a giant snowball *down* a hill if that hill was covered in deep, sticky snow. Duane considered abandoning the project, but then he would have left a colossal ice-jam in the path, the exact opposite of his good intentions. So he shouldered into his "companion" and he pushed and he pushed and he pushed some more.

Hours later, they arrived at the Fabulous Beach. His "companion" stood as proud and noble as a monstrous ball of snow could stand. Duane, on the other hand, fell onto his back, very sweaty and tired, and stayed there for a very long while. Of the two, I would say that Duane moved the least.

"Wow," said Duane, in awe of the snowball, which seen from his current angle was blocking the sun and casting a shadow over him.

Eventually he managed to sit up, and soon after, with a few groans, he managed to stand up. Dragging his sore, achy body back to his cave for a nap was what first crossed Duane's mind, but then his heart reminded him of his original commitment, which was to help his friends. I should point out that although Duane's heart was not as loud and demanding as his stomach, it still could get his attention when it felt it was important to do so.

Duane sighed, not out of frustration or longing, and certainly not out of contentment, but out of a knowing that what he had to do would not be easy or even fun, but it would be vital, so best get on with it. Handsome's field was presumably next in line for snow removal, but Duane thought of Twitch and her burrow. *She might be in greater need,* he thought. *Best clear her place first, and then finish off with Handsome's.*

The polar bear slogged and plodded through the thick snow toward the river at the wide point below the waterfall. Duane wished he could belly-slide across the frozen water, as was his custom in the winter months, but the snowfall was just as copious here, so it thwarted even that small bit of fun. Thus more slogging and more plodding, interspersed with grunting and groaning, all the way across the frozen river and then up to the hilly meadow where Twitch's burrow was usually found.

But where was it exactly? The meadow was nothing but a smooth pane of white interrupted by only the faintest of slopes and curves. Duane scratched his head. Then he squinted and scrutinized the landscape. *Was the burrow there? Or there?* he wondered.

"Twitch!" Duane shouted. "Can you hear me?"

Somewhere, beneath the snow, a muffled voice

responded. "Hear you loud and clear, Duane. My ears are quite sharp, not much that doesn't get heard, just saying."

Duane heard the sound, but not well enough to understand. "Was that you, Twitch?"

"Thought I made that clear, I did refer to you by your proper name, and I can't imagine too many other creatures in this part of the meadow other than myself presently, as the Major is on his migration. Wouldn't mind neighbors, though, if they're friendly, not too noisy, not in the habit of constant renovating, just saying."

Duane didn't understand any of that, either, nor could he tell exactly where it came from, but he had located the general area. As it did sound like a voice, it stood to reason that it was Twitch's voice, since Duane knew of no others who lived in the meadow. Those of you with keen eyesight and reading skills will realize that is basically what Twitch had just said in the last paragraph.

Duane delved right into the task at hand. Another snowball was made, but this time he rolled it this way and that way, randomly clearing the snow in search of the burrow's entrance. When he eventually stumbled upon the door, the meadow resembled a maze of haphazard corridors more in keeping with Magic's tunnel system. He knocked on the door, and Twitch quickly emerged.

"Hello, Duane," said Twitch. "Nice to put a face to the voice, ooh, and look, you've cleared some space in the meadow. So it's day, is it? Quite bright, lost track of time, there in the darkness beneath the snow. Enjoy the gift of sunlight, I do, thank you for that, Duane, and the lack of suffocation, just saying. Who's your stout friend?"

This time, Duane understood right away that Twitch was making a joke about the large ball of snow he ended up creating while in his search for her whereabouts. "Yes, my *friend*," Duane snickered, and then winked to let Twitch know he got the joke. However, Twitch was not making a joke. After days of darkness in the covered burrow, her eyes were blinded by the sunlight, and she truly did think Duane wasn't alone.

"Well, my *friend* and I should be off," said Duane,

continuing the joke. "We are going to clear a path for you across the stepping stones and down to the Fabulous Beach."

Twitch watched awhile as Duane pushed the large snowball down the meadow in the direction of the stepping stones. "Doesn't talk much, that new friend of his," she muttered to herself. "And look how he depends on Duane to move forward. That is someone in need of some rigorous cardio-hopping, just saying."

As before, the snowball Duane pushed grew bigger and bigger the more distance he rolled it. By the time he crossed the river, it was already as tall as the "companion," and by the time he pushed it down to the Fabulous Beach, the "friend" made the "companion" look puny. Smaller still was Duane, whose limbs were so tired from the straining effort, he could barely lift them. "I'm really not a polar bear built for snow removal," he told his new "friend" and "companion." He headed up the path toward his cave for a well-deserved rest.

Whereas Duane had completely forgotten his offer to help Handsome, the musk ox most assuredly had not. "Ah, there you are," he said to Duane, who was shuffling past. "I began to wonder if you'd ever show up."

Duane turned his head toward Handsome's field. At this point, head-turning required more effort than you might realize, so achy was Duane's body. He took in the size of the field and the depth of the snow, and then he sighed loudly. It wasn't a sigh of sadness—well, maybe a little. It wasn't a sigh of frustration—well, there was probably some of that, too. It wasn't a sigh of disappointment— although in truth, how could there not be a lot of that? It definitely was not a sigh of contentment, so overall, in whatever mix, it was an unhappy sigh.

"Problem, Duane?" asked Handsome.

The polar bear was about to say that yes, there was a problem. He was about to say, *Sorry, I can't help right now because I badly need a rest.* But before those words were spoken, Duane's heart spoke to him first, reminding him again of his obligation. Even with his stomach speaking to him at the same time, and more loudly, on the topic of meals before rests, it was still his heart that Duane listened to.

"No problem, Handsome. I'll get right to it."

Much more slowly than before, Duane made his third ball of snow and began rolling it up and down Handsome's field, leaving a lower and more manageable snow level wherever he went. For those of you readers and listeners who have witnessed lawn cutting where you live, you will recognize that Duane was doing almost the exact same thing, if you replaced summer with winter, grass with snow, and used a humongous snowball instead of a lawn mower.

"Thank you so much, Duane," said Handsome, visibly relieved by the results. "You have lightened my mood and eased my movement."

Considering how tired he was, and considering the fact that his work wasn't completely finished yet, it's remarkable that Duane found the energy to attempt a joke. "Don't thank me; thank my *buddy*," he replied, putting his paw around the snowball.

"Yes, amusing," said Handsome charitably.

Fortunately, the snowball Duane had to roll down to the Fabulous Beach after taking care of Handsome's field was big, but certainly not "friend" big, or even "companion" big. The "buddy" was only Duane-big, and Duane pushing it down to the Fabulous Beach did not make it grow much larger because the path had already been cleared. Better still, with no sticky snow left along the path, there was no extra effort required to move it. Duane was so grateful that his last act of helpfulness would be the easiest. He pushed a bit, the "buddy" rolled a bit, he pushed a bit more, the "buddy" rolled a bit more and then a bit more and a bit more, suddenly gaining both speed and independence as the distance grew between it and Duane. Down the hill the "buddy" rolled, past the snow-covered berry bushes, toward the Fabulous Beach. Duane chased after it, more out of curiosity than anything else.

As it turned out, C.C. was already on the Fabulous Beach looking up at both the "companion" and the "friend." Throughout the day, she'd been following Duane's Herculean efforts, using her telescope on the bow of the Shipwreck. The wise snowy owl was almost tempted to fly over earlier to guide Duane on how to build a shovel, but then the snowball-pushing was proving such a useful demonstration of the laws of friction that, for research purposes, she let it play out. C.C. might have reconsidered that decision had she known that at that moment, a third large snowball named the "buddy" was hurtling toward her from behind.

"Look out, C.C.!" yelled Duane, who had only just spotted her on the Fabulous Beach and could plainly see the oncoming collision about to happen.

Then C.C. turned her head a hundred and eighty degrees and could also plainly see what was about to happen.

Perhaps this is the wrong time in the story to discuss the five laws of friction. And to be honest, I am probably not the most qualified narrator to talk on the subject. Friction involves stuff like surface areas and perpendicular forces and knowing which topics are best avoided at the dinner table . . . I think. But what I can say is that in this situation, there was very little friction at play to slow down the large snowball and prevent it from literally bowling C.C. over.

In those seconds before impact, one can only imagine what thoughts were going on in C.C.'s head. It might have been about the fragility of life, or the fleetingness of time, or about how much less traumatic it is to observe science from a distance than to have science smack you straight in the face.

Yet those deep thoughts were all for naught, because the coming catastrophe didn't happen. Yes, the "buddy" was coming at her, but just behind the "buddy" was Duane, running as fast as he could. Duane, who was so achy and so tired, ran to save C.C.'s life. He ran and then leaped onto the runaway snowball. For a good twenty to thirty revolutions, they were inseparable, Duane and the "buddy," one rolling over the other over the other and so on. They were a blur of fur and ice from C.C.'s perspective. But then a polar bear leg stuck out from the speeding snow-ball, followed quickly by a second leg. Both legs stiffened and p r e s s e d hard against the ground. The snowball stopped rolling. It skidded instead. Still rushing toward the beach, still coming directly at C.C., the large, unrolling ball of snow carried Duane backward as he hugged it with outstretched arms, pushing his legs hard into the earth, slowing it only slightly, but then slowing it slightly more . . . and slightly more . . . slowing it . . . slowing it . . . s l o w i n g it until finally, the "buddy" came to a stop.

Duane sighed.

C.C. sighed.

I, your narrator, definitely sighed.

In all three cases, it was a sigh of relief.

Had C.C. recounted this episode to you, I expect it would have sounded far less dramatic. She did thank Duane afterward for preventing what could have been a terrible injury. She thanked him curtly, as is her way. She also followed the thank-you with a long lecture on the different laws of physics that were on display: friction, naturally, but also Newton's laws of motion, forces working against other forces, and so on. I think C.C. was actually quite shaken up from the ordeal, and talking about science, from a distance, was a way to calm herself down. To be honest, neither Duane nor I was listening with rapt attention. I have no excuse, but in Duane's defense, he had simply spent the last bit of energy he had to give.

"C.C., I think I've done enough snow removal for today, or perhaps for this lifetime. I'm off to bed now."

There was no objection coming from his heart this time as Duane made his way up to his cave and crashed onto his soft mattress, having already fallen asleep before his head hit the pillow.

A lot happened during Duane's well-deserved nap. With the paths cleared and movement unconstrained, Duane's friends were free to meet, and eventually they all did, down at the Fabulous Beach. In their conversations, there was talk of Duane's helpfulness. When C.C. told the others about the near-fatal incident, they all realized how heroic his kindness could be.

"Kindness like that deserves a tribute, it does," said Twitch.

"Yes," agreed Handsome, "a monument in recognition."

A thoughtful pause followed as all the friends— Twitch, Handsome, Magic, C.C., and even Boo— considered Duane's good qualities, there on the

Fabulous Beach, where they stood among three extremely large snowballs.

I cannot tell you when the first snowman was invented. Even C.C.'s books do not hold that information within their pages. But I can tell you when the first snowbear was made, and I all but guarantee than any snowbears that have been made since have not come close to the size of this one.

It is no small task to put a gigantic snowball onto a colossal snowball and then put a Duane-sized snowball at the very top of both. It involves pulleys and ropes and Sun Girl's sled and the Pack's demonstration of teamwork. It involves yet more lectures on physics from C.C. and Handsome's deep understanding of art. It involves Magic climbing up to the top to make Duane's face, to sculpt his ears, to carve his gentle smile and fill in his soft eyes. It involves Twitch using food coloring to fill in the features as necessary. It requires Magic to go up again, after everyone else complained, and remove Twitch's mixing bowl that Magic thought would make a funny nose. It entails Boo using her antlers to scratch out a simple message of gratitude at the base of what they created together.

Once it was completed, Duane's friends did not tell him. They decided to let Duane discover it on his own.

The next morning he awoke, feeling much better after a rejuvenating rest. Still half asleep, Duane got up, pulled off an icicle pop from the mouth of his cave, and lazily stumbled and slurped his way along the cleared path, down to the Fabulous Beach for a bit of sun. Obviously, he could see the thing before he arrived, as it was so big. But seeing and understanding are two different things. Closer and closer Duane came, while his eyes grew bigger and his jaw dropped. *That's me!* he thought, marveling at the snow statue now towering over him. *Look at me. I am a giant! As big as a mountain!*

At the base of the monolithic snowbear, a short, simple message: *Thank you for being you, Duane.*

Need I tell you that Duane was touched by this

gift? Surely not. But it wasn't just that the snowbear was so big that made an impression on him. For Duane, it was knowing that the snow that formed his likeness was snow he gathered from the paths leading to his friends, and in so doing, they were all connected to him in a meaningful way.

Duane sensed he was no longer alone. He looked to his left, saw no one, and then he looked *down* to his left. The weasel was standing next to him, sneering as usual.

"It won't last, you know. Eventually, it will melt."

Duane wasn't mad or hurt. He smiled at the weasel sympathetically and nodded. "As it should be. A polar bear such as myself doesn't want to have a big head forever."

But in the meantime, until the seasons changed and the sun grew stronger, there would be Duane, larger than life, made of three huge snowballs named the "companion," the "friend," and the "buddy."

9.
A CERTAIN PUFFIN IS LATE, A CERTAIN ARCTIC HARE IS WORRIED, AND ALL HER FRIENDS ARE UNCERTAIN WHAT TO DO

DUANE KNEW IT HAD come as soon as he stepped on the Mainly Frozen Ocean and it felt like a slightly slushy ocean. For Handsome, it was discovering a saucer-sized hole in the winter ice that covered his pond that was just big enough to reflect back his nose. The tingle of growing antlers was what tipped off Boo. C.C. simply consulted her star charts. But for Twitch, she felt it deep in her heart, a faint vibration that would grow into a tremor. Spring had finally arrived, and for her it meant Major Puff was soon to follow.

What Twitch did not realize was that Major Puff hadn't left on his migration as early as she and the others had assumed; everyone, that is, except Duane, who had found the puffin hiding in a cave, reluctant to fly off. That delay in departure pushed back the date of his return. So as the days passed, each one getting slightly longer and warmer than the previous, Twitch grew ever more worried.

Having never migrated herself or even flown in the sky above the mountains and oceans, Twitch was left to invent the Major's journey as she imagined it. "An easy breeze on his tail feathers, clear views all around," she told Handsome early on in the new season. Against her better nature, Twitch took on a decidedly positive attitude. "Plenty of resting spots along the way, friendly fellow travelers to point him in the right direction. Wouldn't you agree?"

"Hmm? Yes, no doubt," Handsome replied,

somewhat distracted, as he was busy scrutinizing his nostrils for nose hairs. Peering into the only exposed water in his frozen pond was challenging. It required him to stick his neck way out in order to see his reflection. "Am I mistaken or have I grown stubble over the winter?"

"Never mind that!" yelled Twitch in a tone also not in sync with her better nature. "Did you hear a word I said, Handsome?" Twitch stared at him five seconds longer than was comfortable for the musk ox. This, in turn, made Handsome feel defensive.

"Yes, Twitch, I heard every single word. 'A wheezy sneeze, mail letters, cashier shoes all in brown, plenty of forget-me-nots on a tray, twenty cello dabblers with a slight infection.' There, you see? I was listening. Satisfied?" Handsome returned the harsh stare back at Twitch, feeling vindicated. But as Twitch continued to fume and glower, Handsome began going over the list of nonsense that he had just spouted and quickly realized he couldn't have possibly heard correctly.

Twitch hopped off upset, which in turn made Handsome indignant.

"Well . . . it's your own fault for telling me things! I am notoriously bad at listening. I often don't."

A week later, Twitch's positive mindset began to sour. "Perhaps those gentle breezes were more like hurricane gales," she fretted to C.C. at the Fabulous Beach. "Maybe he couldn't find a place to put his feet up. Hard on the lower back, all that wing flapping, I imagine. Nice to find a soft spot along the way, like a tuft of moss or a sofa, just saying."

Had Twitch been more awake during the informal get-together she hosted for C.C. back in the autumn, she would have known that C.C. was undoubtedly the wrong friend with whom to share her worst fears as they pertained to migrations. Rather than putting Twitch's fears to rest, C.C. blithely woke them up with descriptions much more terrible.

"Hurricanes are certainly a possibility," the

snowy owl agreed. "Those winds can pack a powerful wallop. And if Major Puff is blown off course, there is no saying how long it might take for him to find land to rest his wings. Eventually he will tire and plunge straight into the frigid water."

Twitch's front paws went straight to her mouth to stifle a gasp of shock.

"Now, could Major Puff then float for a while, allowing him to catch his breath?" C.C. conjectured, allowing a ray of hope in Twitch's darkened imagination. "Not much of a rest if the waves are churning about, constantly forcing him under the sea. The outcome does not look good. And to make matters worse, my weather calculations indicate a period of fog over us soon, making it near impossible to discern a familiar landmark."

In less than three seconds, Twitch's face went from stone-blank stunned to drooping in utter misery to collapsing on the verge of tears until finally, her anxious, frustrated feelings exploded. "You're not helping at all!"

Twitch hopped back to her burrow and, for the time being, decided it would be easier on the nerves if she stayed on her side of the river and fretted by herself.

Time passed. Winter thawed. The Major remained unarrived. It seemed that none of the friends understood the gravity of the situation in the way that Twitch understood it. They kept tabs on her but only from afar, fearing another outburst. What they saw disturbed them greatly.

During this period of worry, Duane had been deeply engaged in one of the longest naps he had ever had the pleasure of succumbing to. Perhaps that hint of springtime, when his paw touched the slushy ocean ice, convinced him to get in one last luxurious sleep before the warmer weather awoke in him the desire for more active pursuits. It was his empty stomach that put an end to it, grumbling in complaint and suggesting that a humongous post-nap brunch was in order to make things right. But when Duane finally did open his eyes, and kept them open, there was evidently a lot to catch up on, besides meals. Staring down at him, at a distance that one might call "overly intimate," were the alarmed faces of Handsome, C.C., and Magic. Duane blinked back, confused.

"How can you be napping during a time like this? I mean, really!" exclaimed Magic, getting the ball rolling.

Handsome immediately jumped in. "Our friend has likely gone 'bonkers'—to use a medical term— and yet you selfishly take this occasion to 'wallow in sloth'—to use a literary term."

C.C. was equally agitated. "Duane the polar bear, as you know, I am an owl committed to reasoned, thoughtful speculation, but Twitch's irrational behaviors are, without a doubt, off the charts, or at least they would be if such charts existed, which they do not, but I'm working on it."

Still groggy from his extended nap, Duane responded with less alarm than his accusers had hoped to arouse. He sat up and quietly asked, "So this is about Twitch, then?"

"Duane, Duane, Duane," groaned Magic while crumbling to the ground very dramatically. "Try to keep up!"

To that end, Duane's friends dragged him out of his cave, over to the river, then across it and straight to the meadow beside the burrow to witness firsthand the demise of Twitch's sanity. Sadly, the post-nap brunch that Duane had imagined himself feasting on would not be happening anytime soon. He resigned himself to that sad situation, but his stomach did not. It growled its displeasure the whole way there.

The four friends, as well as the one unfriendly stomach, reached the meadow's edge. Duane took in the fact that spring had indeed arrived during his sleep, because the grasses and plants and flowers were now well into their growing period, while at the same time, the snow was melting and thinning into separate patches.

"There she is!" whispered Magic loudly. She spotted a pair of long ears bouncing atop the hill's crest. "Everyone, get down and hide!"

This was easier said than done. Whereas hiding was a simple affair for Magic and C.C., for Duane and Handsome, who were much larger, hiding amounted to basically lowering their heads and imagining themselves to be very, very thin. But they needn't have worried. Twitch was far too occupied with what she was doing to pay any attention to them, even as they slowly advanced for a closer look.

"What *is* she doing?" Duane wondered aloud. What he witnessed was Twitch hopping around the meadow in a large circle. But it wasn't just hopping; it was more like hop-stomping. The arctic hare was tramping down the newly grown grasses and plants, crushing them flat, as she completed her arc.

"That's what I've been trying to tell you!" whispered Magic loudly and again, overdramatically. "This is exactly the issue we have had to contend with, day after day, while you did nothing but snore and snort! I mean, really!"

Magic was getting somewhat carried away with her scolding, for in fact she and the others did nothing more than what they were presently doing, namely observing their friend hop-stomping. Duane ignored Magic's rant and focused instead on Twitch. "Is she angry at the plants?" he asked. "I thought she liked plants."

"I posed the same question, Duane the polar bear," said C.C. "But as you will soon see, Twitch crushes one large circle of flora, then crushes another smaller circle within it, and finally a third circle in the middle."

"Why would she hate some plants but not the others?"

"Exactly," said C.C., nodding and notably impressed with Duane's improved lines of inquiry.

"She repeats this every day, while spouting some incantation," Handsome added. Duane was about to say that he didn't know what spouting an incantation meant, but Handsome anticipated the question. "Which means, Duane, that Twitch is reciting a spell over and over as she stomps her destructive path."

Duane's eyes grew very, very big as he gasped in shock. "You mean . . . magic?"

"Me?" asked Magic.

"No, sorry, not you," Duane clarified, "but *magic* magic?" His eyes grew very big again.

"Oh, please!" said C.C., whose eyes, which are always big, now rolled in annoyance. A short pause followed as all eyes, big or otherwise, turned toward C.C. in disbelief. For the first time, as far as Duane, Handsome, and Magic could remember, C.C. had voiced an opinion that sounded, well, snarky. C.C. noted their shocked reaction and, truth be told, felt secretly proud of herself. "Could we please forgo any talk of magic?" she asked nicely.

"It shouldn't be discounted," argued Handsome. "Listen to her."

They all sidled closer to hear. Aided by a breeze that carried Twitch's voice toward them, what was heard certainly sounded mysterious and even mystical.

"Feel bad but it's for the greater good." *Hop-stomp*. "Feel bad but it's for the greater good." *Hop-stomp*. "Feel bad, truly bad, just saying, but it's for the greater good." *Hop-stomp*.

"There. See?" said Handsome with a confident grin. Like C.C., he was feeling secretly proud of himself because on this occasion he actually *had* been listening. "How do you explain that?"

"I can't," C.C. admitted. "But without a doubt, without a subatomic fraction of a doubt, it's *not* magic."

The owl and the musk ox had to agree to disagree, or at least, that is what Handsome told himself, and the whole group returned to the other side of the river, silent and deep in thought.

"What if . . . ?" said Duane, suddenly. "What if she isn't bonkers?"

"Interesting theory," Handsome responded sagely. "Go on."

"Well . . . she's all alone in the burrow while Major Puff is away on migration. Perhaps she is sad and lonely. And if she is sad and lonely, then—"

"I think I see where you are going with this," Handsome interrupted, his voice getting markedly excited. "If she is sad and lonely, then what she needs is—"

"A party!" Magic screamed.

"Indeed!" shouted Handsome. "You snatched the word right out of my mouth!"

The word Duane was about to say was "hug." Twitch might just need a hug, *not* a party. But good luck trying to tell his two friends that.

"Duaney-Duane (*poke, poke*), that was a brilliant idea," said Magic. "We'll sing songs, and play games, and pull tricks on one another! Probably play tricks more than the songs and other stuff."

"And I shall prepare a tray of delicious delights," said Handsome. "Watercress sandwiches, scones and jam, macarons for those so inclined—all served with aplomb."

Duane and C.C. stood silently, watching Magic and Handsome work themselves up into a frenzy of party planning. In all issues of a social nature, C.C. remained bewildered and felt out of her depth. As for Duane, he wasn't thrilled by the idea of a party as much as you might have imagined, despite it involving food. Having encountered aplomb at his first afternoon tea party hosted by Handsome a while back, he was somewhat underwhelmed by its taste.

"Invitations must be made and sent out at once," Handsome insisted. "Shall this be a formal affair or costumed?"

"Let's tell some that it's formal and others that it's costumed. That way no one will know who made a mistake!"

"Ho-ho! Wickedly clever. Well done. Next topic—decorations."

Duane and C.C. turned and looked at each other. C.C. shrugged her shoulder feathers and flew home. Duane followed her example and headed home too. Magic and Handsome were too involved in their arrangements to notice either's absence.

Back in his cave, Duane's thoughts were still on Twitch. He was genuinely worried about her. For as long as he had known Twitch, she was always ready to lend a paw or make an occasion more special with a nibble, and she never asked or expected something in return. Whether Twitch was presently just sad or whether she was deeply troubled, it seemed to Duane that the least he could be was understanding.

So the next morning, he returned to the meadow. He hoped to have a chat and to offer comfort, but this time, instead of finding Twitch hop-stomping, he found her engaged in something equally bizarre. The arctic hare was going around the meadow and pulling out all the colored flowers she could find. Each time she did so, another incantation followed.

Pull-snap. "Feel just awful, but for the greater good." *Pull-snap.* "Feel just awful, but for the greater good." *Pull-snap.* "Feel awful, woozy with the guilt, just saying, but for the greater good."

Over and over, Twitch repeated this rite, filling her front paws with colored flowers. When she could hold no more, she hopped over to the stomped-down circles of grass and began spreading the flowers over them. Then back to the flowers for more pull-snapping and regrets. Duane could not make heads or tails of it, but rather than avoid Twitch, as Handsome, Magic, and C.C. had been doing, Duane let his heart guide him closer.

Pull-snap. "Feel just awful, but—"

"Hello, Twitch," Duane said, drawing her attention. He followed his greeting with a warm smile, but in return, Twitch gave him a look he'd seen from her only once before, back when they first met. It was a serious look that said, in no uncertain terms, that she was not to be trifled with.

"Hello, Duane, nice to see you up and about, no time for chatting, work to be done, goodbye."

And with that, he was dismissed. Duane meekly turned to leave, but his heart spun him around again. "May I help you with your work?"

Twitch hesitated before answering. Her eyes darted back and forth as she weighed the pros and cons. "Thank you for the offer, lots of work, could use the help, four paws better than two and time being of the essence—but! No talking, Duane, no chatting about storms or casual comments about drowning, my nerves can't handle it. Understood?"

Duane had no intention of bringing up such topics. Nonetheless, he nodded solemnly that he understood, but then he spoke anyway. "What about the incantation?"

"The what?" Twitch asked.

"You know—'sorry about pulling you out, feel awful, for the greater good'—that thing?"

Twitch suddenly appeared to relax. She gave

Duane a small, affectionate smile. "Incantation is optional, but would be greatly appreciated, thank you, Duane, feel terrible, I do, about it all."

With that, the two friends spent the rest of the morning pull-snapping the colored flowers, making apologies, and filling in the three circular ruts. Duane did not ask Twitch even once what the end purpose was. He accepted that whatever it was for, it was important to her and he could see upon completion that Twitch looked noticeably relieved. He silently took his leave while she preoccupied herself with looking up at the sky.

As I may have mentioned once or five times earlier in these stories, Duane was a polar bear in possession of a curious nature, which meant that by the time he reached the river, the not knowing what he helped Twitch complete got his thoughts churning. *Is it some kind of game?* he asked himself. *No, Twitch was in too serious a mood for games. Wait! Perhaps it's a garden.* He'd seen a picture of a garden in one of C.C.'s old books. Like Twitch's circles of flowers, the garden kept plants in an orderly fashion. Quickly, Duane dismissed that theory. *Gardens are for growing plants. Twitch and I, with all our pull-snapping, were doing the opposite of growing them.* Walking nimbly across the stepping stones of the river, Duane had another series of thoughts, equally as nimble. *Twitch was looking up at the sky when I left. Why was she looking up? There was nothing there, not even clouds. Oh my, imagine if there were someone up there, looking down at Twitch and me doing what we were doing? Imagine what they would see.* Then Duane stopped and tried to imagine what "they" would see. He couldn't. There were limits to his nimbleness. But a new and important question came to him instead. *What if whatever Twitch and I were doing was actually meant for someone to see from up there all along?* And that was when Duane reached the other side of the river and found himself at a crossroads, so to speak. He could either head to the Shipwreck and ask C.C. to fly over and give him a report, or he could continue past his cave and walk up Baby Whaleback Hill, with its panoramic view, and see it for himself.

You might think that the obvious choice would be the latter. After all, a firsthand account is generally better than a secondhand one. But some of you may remember that the last time Duane had gone up Baby Whaleback Hill, which really is more of a mountain than a hill, he did not have a great experience. There were some unpleasant bits involving sliding down the hill on a toboggan at a reckless speed, then launching up into the sky at a ridiculous height, followed by plummeting to a hard, unforgiving ground. So while Duane did want to go up and see for himself, at the same time, he was hesitant.

But I won't be tobogganing down Baby Whaleback Hill today, he reasoned. *I will simply walk up the hill and return the same way. Unless I accidentally slip onto a toboggan that happens to be lying around, I should probably be fine.*

Convinced that the odds of surviving were in his favor, Duane made his way to the hill's base and began the long hike up. The higher he went, the more of the Very, Very Far North he could take in. The more landmarks he saw and recognized, the less worried and more happy he grew. He spotted his cave and Handsome's field, he caught sight of the Shipwreck, and he saw the river in the distance. Beyond the river was the meadow. Within the meadow was the thing he helped Twitch complete. Even from far away, it was easy to spot. The three rings of multicolored flowers stood out from the rings of green grass. It was eye-catching. It was beautiful. *But what is it?* Duane still wondered.

10.
A FRIEND OFFERS HELP IN TIME
FOR THE MAJOR'S RETURN

"I SEE THAT TWITCH has made a target."

The voice that spoke from behind Duane made him jump in surprise. He was so grateful that there weren't any toboggans nearby to accidentally step on. When he caught his breath and his balance, he turned to discover Sun Girl and the Pack. "Hello, everyone," he said. "Would you please repeat what you said that Twitch made?"

"A target," Sun Girl explained. "Something to aim for."

"Something to aim for . . ." Duane's thoughts were churning again. *Target. Seen from above. Twitch. Lonely and sad. Major Puff. Away on migration. He left late. He still hasn't returned yet. Oh! She wanted to make sure he finds his way home. So . . . give him a target!*

"It won't work, though," said Sun Girl, pulling Duane out of his musings. She and the Pack looked up and studied the sky. "Sea fog will be coming in soon. It will be thick. Major Puff won't see the target the way it's been built now." The Pack nodded in agreement.

Duane took in the gravity of the situation. All this time, Twitch had not been sad; she was just worried. But if Major Puff does return soon, the fog will hide the target and he won't see it. He might get lost or maybe even injured. "Is there anything we can do?" the polar bear asked.

Sun Girl came up to Duane and gently took his

paw. "Yes, there is, but we'll need to head south first toward the tree line to pick up some supplies." Side by side, with the Pack in tow, the girl in the red parka and the polar bear made their way down Baby Whaleback Hill. Knowing that there was a plan of action, Duane felt reassured enough to change the subject and ask why Sun Girl and the Pack were atop Baby Whaleback Hill in the first place.

"We were having a renaming ceremony," Sun Girl explained.

"We had a vote," added seven of the eight members of the Pack in unison. "Baby Whaleback Hill is really more of a mountain, so that's what we're calling it now."

"Baby Whaleback Mountain *is* fitting," agreed Duane, who considered himself an expert on giving names.

The eighth member of the Pack, who was responsible for the original, not-so-fitting name, reluctantly agreed. And I, your narrator, will less reluctantly refer to it as Baby Whaleback Mountain from now on too.

So at this point in the story, Duane is heading south to the tree line to pick up some supplies; Twitch is standing next to the target made of colored flowers, looking up at the sky and fretting about the Major and the weather; Handsome and Magic are busy planning a party that isn't needed; and C.C. is on the Shipwreck, most likely already distracted with some new subject of inquiry. With all these characters so engaged, I believe our focus should shift now to Major Puff. After all, were it not for him and his long-awaited return, none of the events I've just described would have come to be. The Major would be back in the burrow, Twitch would be calm, and the grasses, plants, and flowers would have had an easier time of it, to say the least.

Doubt me if you wish, but I tell you that Major

Puff was just then on the last leg of his journey home. The trip was grueling, as it should be, considering the distance and the fact that it was a serious migration and not a frivolous holiday in any which way. But there had not been any catastrophic obstacles of the kind described vividly by C.C. What about his navigation, you might ask? Was Major Puff off course? Had he lost his bearings? No, certainly not. His navigation skills, by his own estimation, were nothing short of perfect. As evening approached, he knew exactly where the burrow was, straight ahead, as the crow—or in this case, the puffin—flies.

But then the sea fog came in, as C.C. and Sun Girl predicted. It came in fast and it came in thick. It shuttered Major Puff's view of the Very, Very Far North. It closed in around him like a cold, wet blanket. The Major was not so confident about his navigation skills anymore.

"What dastardly trick is this?" he shouted at no one in particular since he was flying solo. "I have not but arrived at my objective when it is suddenly snatched out from under me!"

I would be less than forthcoming if I didn't mention that the Major briefly suspected this was some new tactic created by his foe, the great black-backed gull. He dismissed the idea quickly. Even great black-backed gulls wouldn't stoop so low as to remove geography.

The situation grew more dire with each passing minute. Concern mounted for the exhausted puffin as he flapped his tired, aching wings through the tangle of vapors, searching for a glimpse of a familiar landmark, like a river or a meadow, or any kind of mark, for that matter, like a target made of flowers, just saying. Major Puff flew blindly in circles. His heart told him he was close, but regrettably it couldn't be any more precise. "Hang in there, Major!" the unflappable puffin rallied himself. "All we need is a sign. Just one sign."

Meanwhile, in the meadow also shrouded in fog, Twitch was in utter despair. She knew the target would be useless now. "What was I thinking?" she scolded herself aloud. "Flowers in a fog? Silly old hare." She felt bad for the Major. She felt bad for all the flowers she had pull-snapped to no good purpose. But I hope that you, dear readers and listeners, will be more charitable. Twitch did the best she could do with what she had available. She didn't just fret and worry. She did *something*, and that is worth acknowledging, even if the results were not up to the task.

"Twitch, was that your voice I heard?"

"Yes, Duane," replied Twitch, whose ears always worked much better than his. "And where are you?"

I need not point out that an all-white arctic hare and an all-white polar bear do not make for ready identification in a thick fog.

"I'm over here," said Duane's voice, but closer now. "I've brought some help."

"You brought some—oh, hello, Sun Girl."

I need also not point out that a young girl in a bright red parka does get seen easier. Sun Girl, along with Duane and the Pack, had arrived with the aforementioned help. It was loaded upon the sled they had all pulled over.

"We saw your target from the top of Baby Whaleback Mountain," Duane said, now close enough to be seen by Twitch. "Sun Girl has something that might be spotted better by Major Puff in the current weather conditions."

All the while that Duane was explaining, Sun Girl and the Pack unburdened the sled of a stack of small logs and branches that they scavenged from the tree line farther south. She directed the placement of all the wood pieces until they created the desired shape. In between, she stuffed twigs and bits of dried moss.

Twitch was skeptical. "Not sure how these things will be seen any better from the sky than the poor flowers I pulled out. And it's getting dark, to make things worse."

"Just wait," said Duane. "It will be magical *but* . . . not magic," he added, just in case C.C. was somewhere in the fog, listening.

Sun Girl kneeled on the ground and took out of her pocket a piece of steel and a piece of flint. She struck the flint with the steel, close to the wood and dried moss. Sparks flew. Fire caught. Flames grew. And then with the help of the Pack, who gently blew on those fragile embers, they spread and spread and spread along the length of the wooden shape.

"Ah," said Twitch, both in understanding and in awe.

"Indeed," agreed Duane, who remembered his first encounter with fire when he met Sun Girl in a snow cave, where he found both shelter and warmth during a terrible blizzard.

"Will it work, Duane?" asked Twitch. Her voice was filled with all the heavy emotions she'd been carrying since spring arrived; all the worry and fear and even love, which can sometimes be heavy too.

Duane knew he couldn't promise something that was beyond his control, but like Twitch and her target of flowers, he worked with what was available:

his optimism. "I hope so, Twitch. I really, really, *really* hope so."

Back up in the sky, Major Puff could not tell up from down in the menacing haze. He'd lost all bearings, and unlike Duane, hope for him was in diminished supply. He was so tired. His wings ached. The exertion was overwhelming. His energy was all but used up. If he should have landed then, and found himself somewhere on the Cold, Somewhat Slushy Ocean, whether in the sea or on an ice floe, he might simply perish on the spot. As a puffin of the military class, and a descendant of generations of heroic puffins whose hasty retreats from battles have long been heralded, the Major didn't fear death. He'd imagined far worse demises than this one. What bothered him, as he continued to fly blindly in the fog, was a regret. It pierced his heart, and yet he wasn't able to put it into words. It was a yearning, more powerful than his respect for honor and bravery. This feeling stayed with him the whole return trip to the Very, Very Far North.

What was it? he asked himself, in what seemed to be his last moments, his wings too tired to flap now. What was it he so yearned for? And then . . . there it was below. A sign, burning through the mist. Not a target of flowers, too subtle for the current situation, but a large arrow aflame, pointing to his burrow. "Yes," Major Puff whispered, as happy and relieved as Twitch would soon be. Willing his sore wings to stretch and spread, he glided down toward home.

Several things then followed in succession, and it left many of the characters confused. In order to leave you less confused, I will relay the events simply as they happened.

Major Puff swooped down onto the meadow, dramatically backlit by the burning arrow for all gathered to see. Twitch immediately gasped in shock and joy, while Duane sighed contently. But before either could say a word, Magic and Handsome suddenly burst out of the fog yelling, "Surprise!" Handsome was carrying a large tray of nibbles, Magic was holding what is often referred to as a "whoopee cushion" (feel free to consult with your parents for a detailed definition), and both of them were wearing bow ties and top hats. Major Puff assumed the party was in celebration of his return. Twitch marveled at how quickly the news of his arrival had traveled. Handsome and Magic, on the other hand, stood speechless and stunned, as if their surprise party had just inadvertently walked into another surprise party.

But before any of *that* could be sorted out, C.C. flew in, all excited. "It's a target! I've just figured out that all along Twitch was making a target!" The wise owl, who was proudly holding diagrams and other visual props that would explain her deductions, took in the surroundings and the awkward silence that followed her announcement. There was Twitch, looking very happy. There was Major Puff, looking very tired but very arrived. There were Handsome and Magic, looking very dapper but also very confused. In fact, they looked just as baffled as she currently felt. "Did I miss something?" she asked.

Twitch took charge at this point. "Not to worry, dear. All's well that ends well, each cloud has a silver lining, when life gives you carrots, make a carrot cake, or just eat the carrots, if you catch my meaning."

No one did catch her meaning, but Twitch was too happy to care. She hopped over to Major Puff, who, in an even greater state of bliss, was displaying a ridiculously large grin. He was home, he was safe, and he was surrounded by friends who truly cared for him. A speech was in order, but in truth, the Major was stunned and speechless. His goofy, loving smile would have to suffice, and in any case, Twitch was deftly handling the occasion.

"I'd like to offer my thanks to Sun Girl and the Pack, and to you, too, Duane, for making things right. You're all welcome to stay in the meadow and finish your strange party, but the Major here is off to the burrow now for a quiet cup of tea and a very long nap."

Duane went over to assist Twitch in getting Major Puff safely to the burrow door. The puffin's recent exertions had left him woozy to the point of toppling over. Still grinning, but with eyes closed, the Major leaned his head on Twitch's shoulder. All the while, Twitch hummed a cheery tune quietly to herself. Fog or no fog, spring was finally in the air.

"Good night, Major Puff," said Duane. "Glad to have you back. Good night to you, too, Twitch."

He turned to join the others at the party among the fog and the fire. I don't suppose he heard what Twitch said next, but I, your narrator, certainly did. "So we're calling Baby Whaleback a mountain now, are we? Fitting, really, I suppose, but could be confusing to some who haven't read the first book, just saying."

And with that, the burrow door closed behind her.

11.
THE WEASEL RETURNS, MAGIC LEARNS A SECRET, AND DUANE DISAPPOINTS HER

THERE WAS A COMMON understanding among Duane and his friends that Boo was shy in the company of others. Public speaking was something she struggled with, managing a volume not much louder than a whisper. Fortunate were the times when Twitch was around; she, with her long, sensitive ears, was able to hear what the timid caribou was saying and would sometimes repeat it to the assembled group if necessary.

Therefore, with so little said and even less heard, Boo remained a mystery.

But not being heard is not the same as being misunderstood, as the situation in this story will illustrate. Aside from the shyness, there was the fact that Boo would frequently not be around for days at a time and then suddenly show up, as if out of thin air, and then just as quickly be gone again. There was no schedule or routine to her comings and goings. There was no explanation given.

The foremost thing that no one knew about Boo was where exactly she lived. For some, it was left unknown out of respect for Boo's privacy (Duane and Twitch), and for others it was for genuine lack of interest (Handsome, Major Puff, and C.C.). However, when it came to Magic, things were different. Magic's curiosity bordered on nosiness. Respecting someone's privacy was a concept that she didn't really grasp. It wouldn't take a lot to push her curiosity to a point that would be disrespectful. And that's where the weasel returns to our story.

The weasel often used Magic's extensive network of tunnels that joined the many entrances of her hillside den. In doing so, the weasel and Magic would on occasion pass each other en route to wherever they were heading. If they had any conversations during these brief encounters, they were of the impolite variety.

"Get out of my way! Coming through!" the weasel might yell.

"Get out of *my* way!" Magic might yell back, knocking the smaller weasel to the side.

It was just that kind of rudeness that warmed the weasel's heart to Magic and suggested to him that he'd found a kindred spirit. That was hardly the case. Magic was not nearly the same as the weasel, yet nevertheless, he still recognized something. *All she needs is a little coaxing,* he decided.

On the next occasion on which the weasel and Magic were approaching each other in a tunnel, the weasel moved to one side to let her pass. But before Magic could go too far, he called out after her, "Hey, you ever notice how that caribou just takes off?"

Magic stopped and turned around. "Huh? Are you talking to me?"

"Yeah, I'm just asking," the weasel continued. "That caribou, where does she go?"

Magic was annoyed by the question. "I don't know where Boo goes. Does it matter? And who are you, anyway?"

The arctic fox turned back in the direction she was heading. She had no time for presumptuous questions from complete strangers in a tunnel she thought was her own.

"Yeah, maybe you're right," the weasel said. "I was just wondering what she was hiding that was so important, that's all."

Magic froze in her tracks like a statue. Her brain did the opposite. It whirled and buzzed and computed a thousand different possible answers to the question 'What was Boo hiding?' Then just as quickly, it shifted from '*What* was Boo hiding?' to '*Why* was Boo hiding it?' *Is it too dangerous?* Magic wondered. *Is it too super fun? Could it allow the wrong types to fly? Does it involve secret paw-shakes? Why isn't Boo sharing it with us?* Magic couldn't help herself. She couldn't let go of the question. It burrowed into her head.

And meanwhile, the weasel scurried off, snickering all the way.

From that moment on, Magic was on the lookout for Boo. She needed to find out the answer, and until she did, nothing else mattered. So Magic camped herself in a spot next to Handsome's field because that was where she'd likely find Boo grazing quietly in a corner.

Three days later, Boo appeared. Handsome, as was often the case, was occupying himself with his own reflection in the pond, all the while regaling Boo with a tragic story about horn-grooming. Magic hid herself lower to the ground and bided her time.

"My great-uncle on my father's side was convinced that a good horn rubbing gave it a pleasant sheen. On one occasion, he found a firm tree—this was down south, you understand—and he began rubbing his horns against the trunk for several hours. But what he hadn't realized was how hard he was rubbing. The tree was slowly being hewn, and before you could say 'timber,' he rubbed right through the trunk. The tree fell atop his lunch, already laid out, ruining any chance to taste the gazpacho, but that's another story."

Boo smiled and left Handsome's field without any fanfare. It's debatable whether Handsome even realized she was there. In any case, when she left, Magic stealthily followed. Whenever Boo stopped and tuned her ears to what she perceived as an unfamiliar sound, Magic would crouch and hold her breath. If Boo turned to look behind, Magic threw herself into a position that blended perfectly with the landscape. In this way, Magic was able to follow Boo along a rocky path high above Duane's cave until she reached the ridgetop, then headed back down the other side. At the bottom was an open meadow, and on the other side was a forest.

Boo walked beside the tree line until she reached a spot where she paused. Boo looked around one final time before squeezing between two trees much closer together than most. When Magic reached that same place, she saw that there were in fact two long rows of trees grown closely together that formed a natural passageway deep into the woods. Slowly and ever so quietly, the arctic fox snuck between the trees, keeping in the shadows of the corridor. Rays of light brightened the grass at the far end, and as Magic got closer, she could hear singing. It was not only beautiful singing, but it was also both loud and bold.

"La la-la, la la-la, la la-la la!"

So that's it! thought Magic. *Boo has a not-so-shy friend that she is not telling us about!*

Advancing closer, Magic discovered that the passageway opened up into a secret clearing in the woods, the perfect home for a shy and private caribou. What Magic did not discover was Boo's not-so-shy friend, and the reason why is that the loud and bold voice belonged to Boo. Even more surprising was that while Boo was happily singing at the top of her lungs, she was also dancing. Beautifully dancing. Carefree yet graceful and expressive, Boo leaped in high arcs, twirled in midair, kicked out her hind legs, and tiptoed *en pointe*. Her antlers prodded the space before her, leading her body into semi-turns in one direction and then in the other, pushing forward, then gleefully bouncing backward. Boo reared up toward the sky, she rolled along the ground, and she scrunched up tight and stretched out like a

bow, all the while serenading the forest with her happy song.

"La la-la, la la-la, la la-la la!"

Oh my! thought Magic, tossing herself up against the far side of a tree trunk. She refrained from gasping or making any sound lest Boo hear her. *Who would have thought? Boo is amazing! Her voice is incredible! Wait till I tell the others!*

Magic scampered down the passageway of trees, across the meadow, and up and over the mountain ridge. She was near bursting with excitement. Mischief was one thing; it came to Magic naturally. But having a secret? Having something that you know that no one else knows? Well, that felt volatile, like a crack of lightning across the sky or a geyser of boiling water and steam shooting out of the earth's depths. Containing that energy was impossible. Magic had to tell someone, and she had to tell them fast. Duane was the closest.

"Duaney-Duane (*poke, poke*)!" shouted Magic, bursting into his cave, as was her custom, and poking him in the belly, as was her custom too. "You will absolutely not guess what I just saw! You won't believe it! You won't guess it! In a million years, you will not guess it! But guess anyway."

"Was it a berry?" asked Duane, taking the intrusion in stride, as was *his* custom. "A very large berry? A large berry that is perhaps ready to eat?"

"What? No! Why would you even guess that?"

"I was hungry," Duane explained simply.

"No. Not a berry. Something to do with Boo."

A worried look fell over Duane's face. "Is she okay?"

"She's better than okay." A huge smile instantly spread across Magic's face. She couldn't contain her secret anymore. "I just spied Boo singing as loud as Handsome snores! And she was dancing, too, Duane. Dancing!"

"Oh my," said Duane, much to Magic's satisfaction. She had finally caught Duane's attention . . . but perhaps not in the way she had hoped. "Did you say that you spied on her?"

Flustered, the arctic fox quickly brushed her front paws in the air back and forth as if to erase Duane's question. "Yes, sure, but that's not the point! Boo was *singing*, Duane! I heard it! And *dancing*! I saw it! It was a big deal! *You* need to see it too!" Then Magic gleefully recounted the story of how she followed Boo from Handsome's field to her forest hideaway.

Again, Duane was not following where she was hoping to lead him in this conversation. "I'm not sure I would want to see something that was supposed to be private."

Magic stood frozen, wide-eyed and stunned by Duane's lack of interest in her secret, while at the same time still vibrating with the excitement *of* the secret. For several seconds she didn't know what to do with herself. Then she did what she usually did. "Oh, come on!" she yelled, throwing herself to the ground dramatically.

"No, it wouldn't be right," said Duane with a small nod of conviction.

And that was when Magic realized that her friends might not see things the same way she did. It would have been so much better had she arrived at the same conclusion as Duane, namely, that spying on friends or anyone is wrong, but what she inferred instead was that her friends were stick-in-the-muds, dull and boring. Without as much as a goodbye, Magic left Duane's cave sulking and headed back to her den.

The weasel was waiting for her when she returned home.

12.
MAGIC GETS SWEPT UP IN MISCHIEF NOT OF HER OWN MAKING

THERE WAS THE WEASEL, leaning up against the wall of Magic's tunnel.

"Oh, it's you," Magic said, none too friendly. "I've had an exhausting, unpleasant day, and I want to be left alone." Magic slumped to the ground, rolled onto her back, draped a paw across her forehead, and sighed with the heaviness that only one so terribly misunderstood could manage.

"Yeah, I get it," said the weasel. "You saw how

talented your friend Boo was, and you know that everyone else would be amazed too, yet no one wants to listen to you."

One of Magic's eyes opened and peeked out from under her draped paw. The weasel got her attention. It's very possible that Magic might have let go of the whole ignored-secret-about-Boo business. For better or worse, Magic was always able to be passionate about something one minute and completely forget about it the next. The weasel seemed to sense this about Magic.

"It's as if they can't even see what you're trying to do," he continued.

Magic sat up, reenergized. "Exactly! You understand—why can't Duane?"

Hearing Magic say that was music to the weasel's ears. "Forget about Duane. You should tell the others your secret."

Magic was hesitant, even pouty. "What if they say the same thing? What if they won't come and see Boo's singing and dancing either? Even though they would be totally surprised and completely amazed! I mean, really!"

"Yeah, I get that," said the weasel sympathetically. "But what if this time you give them a different reason to come and check on the caribou? You know . . . for their own good."

Magic's face brightened up like thin ice sparkling under a blinding sun. "You mean trick them? I like tricks. I'm good at them. And once they see how amazing Boo is, and once Boo sees how impressed we are, they will all thank me, right?"

The weasel smiled but said nothing.

Over the next few days, Magic approached her other friends with tailor-made reasons for them to check on Boo that had nothing to do with the secret she wanted to share.

"I think that Boo may have caught an exotic disease!" she explained to Twitch with much exaggeration. "She shouts out over and over. She's probably in a lot of pain. It causes her to jump in the air in every which direction!"

"Oh, the poor dear," said Twitch while nervously chewing at her paw. "How she contains herself in our company. Never a word of complaint. Stiff upper lip and such. A hot bowl of soup is what she needs. Or a hot water bottle. Or both, just saying."

With Major Puff, Magic took a different approach. While he was out practicing his offensive and defensive marching techniques, she jumped in front of him and marched backward as she spoke. "I can't say for sure, Major, but I wonder if Boo is in contact with the great black-backed gull forces."

"What say you?" demanded the very shocked puffin, breaking stride. "Boo in consort with the enemy? This is a bold accusation, Magic. Where is your proof?"

"All I know is that she maintains a secret base within the woods. I overheard voices that were not typical of the Boo we know . . . or thought we knew.

I mean, really! She could be a double agent!"

Major Puff's orange beak went pale. Charitably, he was still willing to give Boo the benefit of the doubt. "Perhaps she's been blackmailed or compromised in some way. The great black-backed gull is not above the most dastardly deceits. In any case, this must be dealt with decisively."

It took some time to reach C.C. when her turn came next. The Mainly Frozen Ocean being just the Cold, Cold Ocean during the warmer seasons, Magic couldn't walk over to the Shipwreck. Given a choice, like Handsome, she would prefer to avoid any swimming, so instead, she went over to the Fabulous Beach and waited until she saw the sun reflecting off C.C.'s telescope. Then she jumped up and down, waving her paws frantically to get C.C.'s attention. This took more than one attempt. In fact, it took four attempts, because although C.C. did see Magic on the beach the first three times, C.C. didn't heed the call. The reason being that both Magic and C.C. had boundary issues. C.C.

liked personal boundaries, whereas Magic, as I've pointed out, crossed over them frequently. The idea of Magic ruffling through her feathers or poking her in the belly was not an idea C.C. cared for. But by the fourth siting of the arctic fox waving at her from afar, C.C. considered it might be urgent and worth examining. She left the Shipwreck and flew over to the Fabulous Beach.

"What took you so long?" demanded Magic while dramatically letting her paws hang limp to demonstrate her exhaustion from so much waving. "I've been trying to get you to come over for at least a hundred years!"

Showing remarkable restraint, C.C. did not point out the unlikelihood of one hundred years having passed. Instead, she got down to business. "I'm here now. To what purpose do I owe this meeting?"

Magic got right down to it too. "Boo has discovered a plant that gives her powerful abilities. You need to investigate it."

"What kinds of abilities?" asked C.C.

"Oh, uh . . . jumping. It makes her jump really, amazingly, super high! And it makes her voice really loud too!"

C.C. stared at Magic without blinking for several seconds before speaking. "Is that it?"

Is that it? thought Magic. *Is that it? I think up an amazingly scientific reason to check on Boo and she asks me, "Is that it?"* But out loud, Magic said, "I think it makes Boo super amazingly smart. Like *owl* smart."

C.C. ignored the compliment. "Does Boo eat the plant's flower or its leaf?" she asked.

"I'm not sure," replied Magic.

"How long for the plant to take effect?"

"Couldn't say," replied Magic.

"What does the plant look like?"

"Don't know," replied Magic.

"Where does it grow?"

Magic simply shrugged.

Another long, silent pause ensued in which C.C. stared wearily at Magic, and Magic stared unblinkingly back at C.C. with the sweaty, forced confidence of someone who didn't work out her make-believe story as thoroughly as she'd thought. But in the end, C.C.'s scientific curiosity took sway. "I suppose I should investigate," she agreed.

Phew! thought Magic. *And I mean, really!* she added.

When it came to luring Handsome, Magic put her theatrical skills to the test. "It was horrible, Handsome! It was as if Boo had just given up on her fur. *Sob*—it was matted and dirty. It looked ever so dull. I think I even saw—*sob*—food crumbs lodged within it."

"Oh, I think I feel dizzy and need to sit," said Handsome, gasping for breath. As you can imagine, such news hit him hard. "I have shared all my grooming tips with Boo, yet this

should happen? She is still so young. To give up on fur hygiene is not right at her tender age."

"Exactly!" said Magic, pouncing on the opportunity. "You need to get over there and straighten her out."

"Indeed. I will fetch my things and mentally girdle myself for an intervention."

Magic was relieved to see that this was going much more smoothly than it did with C.C., when all of a sudden Handsome stopped and turned to Magic with a suspicious gaze. "Wait one minute here. Duane once lured me to a 'hair emergency' that turned out to be a hoax. This smells oddly similar to that incident."

Magic put her theatrical skills to another test. She held her ground and stared back at Handsome with a hurt yet defiant expression. "Am I the type of fox who would deceive you like that? I mean, really."

Handsome's eyes narrowed as he scrutinized Magic with so much intensity that it made her tail twitch in nervousness. But then in an instant, Handsome relaxed. "I apologize. I must admit that I am not a good judge of character, as I tend to look down on everyone."

So with all her friends on board, with the exception of Duane, whom she'd given up on, Magic gave them precise directions to Boo's forest home and an agreed time to meet. She warned each of them that in order not to startle Boo, they must remain totally silent with absolutely no talking. This had the added advantage of not allowing them to share their very different concerns as it related to Boo's terrible illness or puffin betrayal or scientific discovery or fur catastrophe.

13.
THE WEASEL GLOATS AS DUANE TRIES TO PREVENT A DISASTER

ALL THIS TIME, DUANE had no clue what Magic was up to. He had been kept out of the loop. While all his friends were making their way over the mountain ridge and down the other side, across the meadow and over to the forest, he was in his cave thinking polar bear thoughts.

I do like to sleep, he pondered, *and sometimes, I sleep a lot. And when I sleep, I often dream. But how do I know whether I'm asleep now? How do I know I'm not dreaming about sitting here thinking about sleeping and dreaming? And come to think of it, how do I know I'm a real polar bear and not one being dreamt up by someone else?* Duane rubbed his eyes with the heels of his paws because thinking was making his head woozy.

When he lowered his paws, there was the weasel, who just stood there, smiling up at him. It was not a pleasant smile. It was a smug and arrogant smile, and it was making Duane uncomfortable. "If you're still looking for your food scrap, I haven't seen it," said Duane. "If you would prefer some of my food, I would be happy to share."

The weasel continued standing and smiling. "Naw, I'm good," he finally said. "I saw your friends a while ago."

"Oh?" replied Duane cautiously. "Which ones?"

"All of them. They were heading over to the caribou's place."

Duane's first reaction was a twinge of hurt. He was about to ask why he wasn't invited to Boo's home if everyone else had been. But then it occurred to him that maybe there was more to this. For one thing, he remembered what Magic had told him a few days earlier about spying on Boo, and second, the weasel was still smiling at him in a way that Duane was certain couldn't mean anything good. Duane bent down to look the weasel straight in the eyes. "Did you do something?"

"Me?" said the weasel in mock surprise. "Me? I ain't done nothing! But Magic, well . . . once you plant an idea in her head, there's no stopping her."

Duane's heart skipped a beat. Something horrible was coming, he was sure of it.

"She's convinced all your friends to pay a surprise visit. I can't imagine it going well with that shy caribou." The thought of it made the weasel break out in laughter. "Surprise! Ha-ha-ha-ha!" He bent over and slapped his legs, overcome by the hilarity of what he was picturing.

Duane now understood that this was a game the weasel was playing, but it was a mean game, which only the weasel got to enjoy.

The weasel stopped grinning. "I told you, *Duane*. Things can go bad in a snap."

Duane suspected that things *could* go bad if they were encouraged to do so. *Poor Boo*, thought Duane. Surprising her would be like touching C.C. or pretending you saw a great black-backed gull standing behind Major Puff. It would be insensitive and unkind.

Duane walked over to his grandfather clock, standing in the corner, that ticked and tocked without hands on its face to tell the time. The clock gave Duane comfort because it could tell him the possibilities of the future. It could tell him what might happen and also what might not happen. "Magic has a good heart," he said to the weasel. "She gets carried away, but she isn't selfish. She isn't mean."

"Maybe yes, maybe no," said the weasel with a shrug. "It doesn't really matter in the end, does it, *Duane*?"

I cannot tell you what motivates someone like the weasel to work so hard to be hurtful. Do they do it out of anger? Jealousy? Fear? I only know that it happens. Duane was beginning to understand that too. If he did have a good life, as the weasel kept sarcastically pointing out, and if he wanted to keep it that way, then Duane would have to protect it, always.

Resolved on that thought, Duane left his cave and followed the directions to Boo's secret home as explained to him by Magic earlier. He went there as quickly as his four legs could run. He went there not knowing for sure what possible outcome awaited. He went there without a plan or any assurance he would arrive in time to change anything. But he went there all the same, because that was where his friends were.

Meanwhile, at the edge of Boo's hidden clearing in the woods, we find Twitch holding a pot of soup, Handsome holding a hairbrush, C.C. holding a magnifying glass, and Major Puff holding a strong suspicion of betrayal. Boo, whom they were all very concerned about, but each for very different reasons, had yet to be discovered. Magic was quietly leading them closer to Boo, using the exaggerated tiptoeing of an arctic fox very caught up in the excitement of her secret.

Then suddenly Boo's voice sang out. It was as loud and beautiful as when Magic first heard it days earlier. The shy caribou, obviously feeling safe in her hideaway, held nothing back in expressing her joyful feelings musically. "La la-la, la la-la, la la-la la!"

The group stopped where they were and listened.

"Oooh, doesn't sound like she's in much pain, if you ask me," remarked Twitch in a loud whisper. "Sounds lovely, she does, like honey to the ears, but not actual honey, if you see my point."

"Shhh!" said Magic, finger to her lips.

The group inched their way closer to the clearing.

"La la-la, la la-la, la la-la la!"

Major Puff was even more affected by the singing than Twitch was. "I find it impossible to imagine that such a beautiful melody, sung with such splendor, could be endured by a conniving great black-backed gull without its wickedness melting away. This is not the voice of a traitor."

"Shhh!" insisted Magic.

The company came right up to the entrance of Boo's hidden clearing. Now they could see Boo move as she sang. The four unintentional intruders were momentarily overtaken by her performance. Watching Boo dance so freely and with such animation was truly spectacular. Mouths and beaks hung open in rapture. But soon enough, confusion settled in, along with a self-consciousness that they perhaps shouldn't have been there.

"Magic, I simply do not understand," said Handsome. "There is absolutely nothing wrong with Boo's fur. Its luster is as magnificent as my own."

"Shhh!" demanded Magic.

C.C. spoke next. "There does not seem to be any plant involved in Boo's behavior. I am not an expert on such things, but if I were to conjecture why she is singing and dancing, it is because she is happy."

"Hmm. Hearing each of our different concerns,

it appears to me that Magic has led us here under false pretexts," said Handsome.

The four friends stared hard at Magic with the implied expectation that an explanation was in order. Magic stared right back, but her resistance didn't last long. "All right, fine! I made some stuff up to get you to come! But it was for your own good because you probably wouldn't have come, and now you did. Now you got to see and hear Boo like we've never seen her. Isn't she amazing?"

"Yes, she is. But we weren't invited, dear," said Twitch in a tone that conveyed her disappointment in Magic. "This was not for us to see."

Magic lost patience. "Oh, come on!" she yelled in her usual overdramatic way, and then, without realizing it, she stepped into the clearing. "Wasn't it worth it? You got to see shy Boo do *this*! This!"

Magic's yelling pulled Boo out of her happy reverie. In mid-leap, she turned her head toward Magic's voice and saw five of her friends standing there uninvited in her secret home, where she felt safe, staring at her doing something that was private, that was not meant to be seen or heard by anyone. Boo gasped in horror. Then she crumbled to the ground, mortified. She hid her face and began to cry.

Instinctually, Twitch, Major Puff, and Handsome gasped too. C.C.'s eyes darted back and forth as she searched for the definition of what she felt, but I can tell you that what she and the others felt was remorse. They were, by no fault of their own, made part of something that caused Boo injury.

Magic still had no understanding of what had just happened. "But what's the big deal?" she said, walking toward Boo. "Right? I mean, really. We all got to hear your amaz—"

"Stay away from me!" Boo shouted, as if shouting was her only defense in the world. She backed away from Magic with terror in her eyes. Her body shook. Her voice flooded with desperation. "Please leave me alone," she whispered. The fear and hurt and true sense of betrayal was all there in those four words.

Twitch and Handsome, C.C. and Major Puff, all bowed their heads in shame. As for Magic, until that moment, she had never considered such a response by Boo and the others. She thought that it would go so much differently, maybe a little blush or a nervous giggle, but nothing more, nothing serious.

Now that Magic saw how Boo did react, she realized she needed to fix the harm she had caused. Magic took another hesitant step forward. "Boo, I want to say I'm s—"

Before her sentence could be finished, Boo bolted deep into the forest and quickly out of sight.

Duane knew he was too late when he heard Boo's pained shout. It had echoed through the forest as he hurried down the passageway of trees. He slowed his run to a walk. Soon he passed Twitch, Handsome, Major Puff, and C.C. heading back. No words were shared. Their embarrassed, concerned expressions said enough.

When he reached the clearing, Magic was still standing in the same place, staring in the direction that Boo had fled. Duane's heart ached for the caribou and he hoped she would be okay, hoped too that they would be able to win her trust again. But in the meantime, there was Magic. Even seen from the back, she looked crushed, her shoulders stooped by the weight of her feelings. Magic was experiencing guilt for the first time in her life. Duane came and stood silently beside her. When eventually she looked up at him, her eyes were red and watery.

"I didn't mean to hurt her," she said, and Duane could tell by how she said it that it was not meant as an excuse but as an acknowledgment that she had indeed hurt Boo.

"I know," said Duane. "We can't fix it now. It will take time. But we will."

Then he placed a gentle paw around her shoulder and led her slowly out of the woods and toward home. The weasel was waiting by the meadow, grinning. Duane shielded Magic from his view, all the while ignoring him as they passed.

14.
EVERYONE IS DEPRESSED, THEN DUANE HAS A HOPEFUL BUT SCARY IDEA

IT HAD BEEN A week and still there was no sighting of Boo. She did not come to graze in the corner of Handsome's field nor linger at the edges of their company. In all that time too, Duane received no visits from Magic. She didn't bounce back from the incident as she might have in the past, acting as if nothing had happened and cheerfully throwing herself into her next mischief. Magic stayed hidden in her den.

A heaviness had fallen over the Very, Very Far North. The other friends hadn't completely forgiven Magic for what she did. But it was more than that. C.C. kept herself overly busy with experiments at the Shipwreck. Whether these were experiments conducted for the benefit of all or for the benefit of giving C.C. a distraction was debatable. Handsome continued staring down into his reflection pond, but his eyes weren't focused on himself. He seemed to be lost in thought. Major Puff had allowed his marching practice schedule to slip, and Twitch didn't have any nervous energy to burn off. Each, in their own way, felt their world had broken somehow, just as the weasel had predicted, if not provoked. Each was adrift.

It would not be fair to say Duane wasn't affected by this gloom. It just wasn't in his nature to succumb to it. Something had to be done, he believed, to bring Boo back, to allow Magic to forgive herself, to help everyone come together again. Duane left his cave and went for a long thinking walk, determined to figure out what to do.

A thinking walk is different from an adventure hike. In fact, it may be the exact opposite. When Duane went out exploring, his mind was focused on his surroundings, tuned to what was out there to see or hear or smell or touch, and open to what might unexpectedly happen and be experienced. A thinking walk demanded that Duane shut out everything around him, allowing his mind and heart to go inward, to concentrate on his thoughts and feelings, to problem-solve. A thinking walk did not require Duane to pay attention to his surroundings other than to avoid walking off a cliff accidentally.

Once Duane got into his stride, the rhythm took over; his heart was beating and his mind was sharp, or at least it was sharper. Duane's thoughts naturally glided toward his friends, about whom he was concerned.

Poor Boo, how terrible it must have been, feeling she was taken advantage of by her friends. It must have felt scary. And now Magic feels awful. Everyone feels awful. Everything is out of balance.

Duane's eyes lit up suddenly. *Yes, balance!*

Duane's thoughts quickly steered toward C.C. in her room at the back of the Shipwreck, among the many books where he learned so many new things. *In one of C.C.'s books, there was a picture of a human walking along a rope high above the ground. It looked very scary. C.C. said it was part of a show. She said it was called a balancing act. That's what we need! We need a balancing act. We need a show for Boo in order to make things right. A show with all of us doing something scary, like it was scary for Boo, but this time she'll watch us, to balance things out.*

And there you have it. Duane's thinking led him to a plan. He would organize an event in which everyone would take a turn doing something they found frightening. He would send an invitation to Boo to come and watch, then hope for the best.

Having an idea is one thing; turning that idea into something real is quite another. In order to do that, Duane would rely on C.C.'s help, as was his custom, so off to the Shipwreck he went, in person this time.

"Hello, C.C.," he said shortly after swimming over and knocking politely on her door. "I would like to share an idea that I've just had on my thinking walk."

The snowy owl gave Duane the kind of unblinking stare he knew would be followed by a question, which it was. "How does a thinking walk differ from your usual walk, Duane the polar bear?"

Inspiration came to Duane a second time. "Ah . . . well, from the outside, you would hardly be able to tell them apart," he replied, surprising even himself with his cleverness.

The answer seemed to satisfy C.C., so Duane proceeded to tell her everything I told you. Because it was a plan involving emotions and feelings—the one subject C.C. might do poorly on during a test if such a test existed—she deferred to Duane's expertise, as was her custom. She also saw the logic of his plan and could offer some useful suggestions. She flipped through the pages of one of her thick books until she came to the picture she had in mind. It was a wooden platform with a long curtain hanging at the back. "This is called a stage. It is used for performances such as the one you've described. I can instruct you on how to fashion one using materials we can scavenge off the Shipwreck."

Duane was delighted. "I could build one of those on the Fabulous Beach. Perfect!"

The next few days were busy for Duane. First he made the rounds to all his friends' homes, inviting them to take part in what he was now calling the Balancing Show. For Twitch, Major Puff, and Handsome, it was readily accepted because it provided a much-needed project to pull them out of their malaise. The idea of doing something scary was equally enticing, although for Twitch, the idea was also . . . well, scary.

"Not sure what I would do," she fretted. "Haven't had much experience in the fate-tempting, reckless, leap-before-you-look department. More of a better-safe-than-sorry, measure-twice-cut-once-do-it-again-just-in-case disposition, just saying."

"I have found C.C. a great source of information on all matters," said Duane. "I suggest you ask her for some help." This was the advice he ended up giving to several of his friends, which in turn led to many unexpected visits with C.C., which in turn allowed C.C. lots of opportunities to practice her chitchat, which in turn led to C.C. considering having a lock put on her door.

When it came to inviting Magic, Duane had to be both gentle and persistent. He approached one of the many, many openings to her den, got down on his stomach, and called out her name. He waited and waited, but there was no answer. He went to the next closest entrance and did the same. Again, Magic wasn't answering. On the third attempt, Duane spoke further. "Magic, it's Duane . . . the polar bear . . . the one you like to poke in the tummy. . . . I know you are in there. Please come out so that I can ask you something. Also, I'm not leaving until you do, so if I end up falling asleep, I apologize for any snoring."

Magic poked her head out slowly. She tried to smile, but her attempt failed dismally, so she quit. "Hi, Duane," she said in a very flat voice. "Any sign of Boo?"

"No, not yet, I'm afraid, but she will show." Then Duane proceeded to explain his idea, and when he was finished, he asked, "So what do you think, Magic? Will you take part? It really needs you for it to work."

Magic wanted to make things right, but she had lost confidence in herself. "What if I end up making things worse again? I do everything too big. I'll probably make a bigger mess."

"You won't. I'm absolutely sure of it." He gave her a smile for encouragement.

Magic was touched by Duane's faith in her, although not convinced herself. "You always say things like that."

"I always mean it," replied Duane.

Building the stage for the Balancing Show was a lot of hard work. C.C. led Duane around the

Shipwreck, pointing to all the materials and tools he would require. Not everything could be found within the storage rooms belowdecks, so parts of the Shipwreck itself were removed to provide the necessary long wooden planks for the stage floor. All of it was then loaded by Duane onto the rowboat, the Wreck-*less*, and in a series of trips was carried over to the Fabulous Beach for construction. Following C.C.'s instructions, Duane sawed and hammered a small platform with a proscenium arch and a curtain backing made of musty old canvas. Being the first time that this particular polar bear attempted an endeavor of this size, the finished product wasn't close to perfect—actually a bit rickety—but would do the trick for one evening.

A few other elements were added to the stage, which Duane didn't understand but which C.C. explained were necessary, and then she mysteriously left it at that.

Major Puff had no idea what he would do for the Balancing Show. Since he came from a long line of military heroes, the chances of him finding any activity that would be scary, if you excluded non-holiday migration, were next to zero. So in search of inspiration, the following morning, Major Puff flew over to the Shipwreck on his own. He and Twitch agreed that in order to keep their performances secret, they should visit separately. The puffin marched down the stairs leading from the top deck of the Shipwreck and began by exploring the various storage rooms. He approached the task with the same tenacity required in finding an adequate burrow, back in the days before he met Twitch. Major Puff rummaged through many boxes, fiddled with this and that, and mumbled to himself about the lack of cleanliness and how, ordinarily, a puffin of his stature wouldn't be caught dead in such a filthy place. There was a lot of banging and clanging as he mucked about, and C.C., who was just down the hall, heard it all. She came over to investigate.

When the two of them laid eyes on each other, there was an awkward pause. To the best of their memories, it was the first time they were ever alone together. C.C. didn't have any chitchat topics prepared, so she was unsure of what to say. Major Puff remembered clearly C.C.'s scary migration facts from the earlier get-together at the burrow and thus was terrified of what she *might* say.

"So . . . ," began C.C.

"Indeed . . . ," replied Major Puff.

They continued staring at each other in complete silence other than a slight creak and groaning of the Shipwreck in the background. Finally, C.C. took charge, if only so she might get back to her studies. "Are you by any chance looking for something for the Balancing Show?"

"Indeed!" replied Major Puff, perhaps too loudly, out of relief. "Your assistance would be invaluable."

So C.C. escorted the puffin through the ship and explained what the different objects were and what they were used for. Surprisingly, it turned out to be an enjoyable morning for them both as they discovered a shared appreciation for machinery and gadgets that do useful, interesting tasks. When they came upon a particular object made of wood and brass, with knobs and gears and such, C.C. needed to demonstrate how it worked in order to explain what it was. Major Puff was so overcome by that demonstration, he requested several more demonstrations. Thus it was now clear to him what his scary performance would be. He set the object aside for Duane to carry over to the Fabulous Beach later. Then he flew to a very private spot where no one could find him or hear him as he created and practiced his piece. For those of you readers or listeners expecting me to tell you what the object was at this point, you will be sadly disappointed. As C.C. might say, it's a wait-and-see situation.

In the afternoon, Twitch arrived. As she was not a confident swimmer herself, Duane pulled her across in the Wreck-*less*. Twitch did not hesitate to visit the snowy owl straightaway, and before she could manage more than a "Hello, dear, would you be so kind as to help me with—" C.C. directed her down the hall to the storage rooms. C.C. had intended to build on her morning success with Major Puff, which was both pleasant and efficient, so she led Twitch on a tour of different scary objects that she might want to consider for her performance. As experiments go, this one did not repeat well. No sooner would C.C. point an item out than Twitch would then grab the nearest thing that could serve as a cloth and give it a good cleaning.

"Can't get a fair look at it if it's covered in grime, filth, and cobwebs, just saying."

The afternoon dragged on and on. C.C. had a twinge of hope that the search might conclude quickly when Twitch looked beyond the selection of scary knives she was being shown and said, "Ah! That's just the thing I need!"

Alas, it turned out to be a whisk broom. Twitch was getting no closer to finding an idea for her performance, but at least the Shipwreck was looking a bit nicer. C.C. finally withdrew to her room at the back of the ship. Twitch was so preoccupied, she didn't even notice.

Hours later, Twitch knocked gently on C.C.'s door and let herself in. C.C. was perched on the table, looking through one of her books. In fact, she was researching what she would need to practice for her own performance at the Balancing Show. The book was one she didn't look through often, as it contained information that C.C. considered whimsical and thus unimportant. The book was not as well kept as her others. The pages had yellowed terribly, and most of them were loose from the binding. And again, if you were expecting that I, your narrator, would tell you the name of the book, then it's just not your lucky day story-wise, I'm afraid.

"What are you looking at, C.C.?" asked Twitch as she approached.

"It relates to my part in the Balancing Show, but in order to keep it a surprise, I cannot tell you more," replied C.C., proving that characters in a story can be just as unhelpful as narrators. Then C.C. removed a loose page and carried it up to the top of a shelf, out of reach, before Twitch could take a look.

Twitch accepted the need for secrecy and focused her attention on the remaining pages of the book, flipping casually through them and commenting as she did. "Ooh, that looks uncomfortable! I imagine you'd need a cup of tea with honey to soothe your throat after trying that. And what on earth is *she* doing? Didn't think that was possible, even if you did a good stretch beforehand. And look at that! Oh my! That's one way to fly, I suppose, if you're not too fussy about loud booms and smoke."

C.C. did not interrupt or crowd Twitch since she was, in her way, doing research, which the snowy owl respected. After some time passed, Twitch saw something in the book that not only seemed right for the Balancing Show, but also spoke to her on a deeper level. "Yes, that's it," she said aloud.

"Did you find what you need?" asked C.C.

"Hmm? Oh . . . yes, I did. And I will be borrowing this page, dear. Promise to take good care of it. Bring it back soon. Not to worry. Need to gather a few items. Saw a chest in the other room. Just give it a quick clean, fill it up with my items, and leave it for Duane to bring back at his leisure. All right, then. See myself out. Hugs and nose twitches."

Swept up in her own energy, Twitch was out the door before C.C. could say goodbye.

When Duane brought Magic over in the early evening, she went reluctantly up to C.C.'s room, knocked on the door, and didn't even come in until given permission. C.C. was pleasantly surprised by Magic's restraint, not comprehending her low emotional state. Magic, too, was relieved that C.C. wasn't making her feel any more guilty than she already did. Rather than talking about what happened with Boo, C.C. got right down to business.

"Do you know what you plan to do for the Balancing Show?"

Magic shook her head.

"Then perhaps I have a suggestion," said C.C. in a tone that was matter-of-fact. "Objectively speaking, you are impulsive, lively, unpredictable, and foolish."

"Okay . . . ," said Magic, unsure where this was going.

"And unlike Handsome, whose self-gazing might be considered excessive, you are someone who does next to no self-reflection."

"Okay . . . ," said Magic again, wondering if she'd just been insulted.

"I believe that this idea will build off your qualities and also be scary for you." C.C. guided Magic to her desk, where the same still-unnamed book used by Twitch was open to a specific page C.C. had already turned to. Magic came closer. She studied the picture but didn't understand what she was looking at. C.C. explained. "And as you can see," she concluded, "nothing is required other than that one small element, which I will create and have ready for you on the night."

So the stage was built, the friends were preparing their performances, and the readers were frustrated by the narrator's withholding of information. All that remained was the invitation to Boo. Duane felt it would be best done in person. He followed the mountain path above his cave, up and over the mountain and then across the meadow to the edge of the forest. When he arrived at the narrow tree opening that led into the heart of the woods, where Boo made her private home, he stopped and called out from where he stood.

"Hello, Boo! It's Duane! . . . The polar bear! I'm just outside the forest, and I'm not coming any farther!"

He waited for a moment. Suddenly, at the far end of the passageway of trees, Boo's head peered out from the side. She took one glance at Duane and quickly pulled her head back out of sight again.

This did not discourage Duane. All that was important was that Boo was there and in hearing range. He continued. "I am here, Boo, to bring you an invitation! I'm not very good at writing like C.C. and Handsome are, so it's more of a yelling situation!" Duane paused again, this time to quickly go over in his head the words he practiced. Then he cleared his throat. "*Ahem* . . . Dear Boo! You are warmly invited to attend the first, and probably only, Balancing Show! An evening of entertainment . . . hopefully! Your friends—who miss you very, very much, by the way—will be performing acts that they have never done before! It will be scary and risky for them, but probably not fatal . . . hopefully! You are not obligated to do anything but watch! It will be held at the Fabulous Beach tomorrow before sunset! We really hope you will come! . . . Okay! That's it! I'm leaving now!"

Duane didn't linger for a response. He turned and headed back to his cave. And as to whether Boo would attend the Balancing Show or not, that too would be a wait-and-see situation.

15.
THE BALANCING SHOW

T HE NIGHT OF THE performance arrived. Everyone gathered before the makeshift stage that
Duane had put together. There was a hum of
excitement. No one had a clue as to what the others
would do that would be scary and daring for them.
Magic did join the group after being so long hidden
in her den. She was not her usual excitable self, but
quite the opposite, quiet and subdued. The others
did not ignore her; each said a polite hello, and she
in turn smiled timidly back. Duane thought Magic

appeared so shy and hesitant, she could have been Boo's reflection. Then, thinking of Boo, Duane looked around, hoping she might have shown up. There was no sign of her yet. *Maybe it was asking too much.* In any case, everyone was getting restless. To Duane's delight, Sun Girl suddenly appeared.

"I heard there was to be a show," she said, sitting next to Duane.

"It's so good to see you, but didn't the Pack want to come?"

Sun Girl shrugged. "I asked them, but they said no. It's a Tuesday. Unexpected things happen."

"Tuesdays," said Duane, nodding in agreement. He stood up to address everyone. Doing so, in the corner of his eye, he caught a glimpse of Boo's face within the shadows at the back, among the berry bushes. *So she came after all*, he thought happily. Duane did not stare, nor did he make any gesture of recognition. He allowed Boo her privacy and instead turned forward to talk. "We should probably begin. C.C. had volunteered earlier to start us off."

The friends sat or perched before the stage where C.C. was now standing next to a blanket that hung from a horizontal rod all the way down to the stage floor. That rod was attached to a vertical rod, like a flagpole, which was weighted at the bottom. C.C. spoke. "As you well know, I am a scientist. I deal with what is. I have no tolerance for frivolous things, like magic, for example." Then, as if it suddenly occurred to her for the very first time, C.C. looked over at Magic and added, "I mean magic with a small 'm,' the act of illusion. Not Magic the fox, such as yourself, whom I *can* tolerate . . . in small doses."

Having straightened that out, C.C. continued. "I, of course, am not scared of magic per se, but I do fear that all of you are prone to believing in it, and there is only so much eye-rolling and lengthy stares that a rational owl such as myself can handle. Therefore, I intend on performing a magic trick while explaining how it's done so you will all be wiser and less shallow."

"Explaining it?" asked Handsome. "That doesn't seem like much fun." Duane had to agree.

C.C. used one of her wings to swivel the blanket to the side, revealing a rectangular, dark wooden frame that contained a series of cylinders holding round, wooden beads. "Beside me is a black, backless abacus."

"A black, backless what?" asked Major Puff, agitated and suspicious.

"An abacus . . . an ancient calculation apparatus . . . a tool to count with."

"Well, why didn't you just say so?"

"I thought I did," said C.C., confused.

"Never you mind him, dear," said Twitch. "You just continue on ruining the magic trick."

"As I shall. Thank you, Twitch." C.C. indicated a portion of the stage floor on the opposite side of her. "I will shortly hide the abacus behind the hanging blanket once again. Then, while you are all distracted, I shall press upon this bit of wood here. When I do that, it will cause a trapdoor beneath the abacus to open slightly, allowing the abacus to slide under the stage and out of sight. When I release my talon from the trigger, the trapdoor closes. Finally, I push aside the blanket, revealing the disappeared abacus."

C.C. was confident that her explanation had sufficiently destroyed any chance of entertaining her audience. She swiveled the hanging blanket in front of the abacus and pulled out a short stick that was wedged beneath her wing. "I now take hold of my *magic* wand, which is not a magic wand, you understand, but in fact just the broken handle off of a chisel I found on the Shipwreck. I say the magical invocation 'abracadabra,' and then I will— Or perhaps before I continue, would you like to know where the word 'abracadabra' derives from?"

"No!" shouted everyone.

"It's just as well, as several theories are in play," agreed C.C., waving her wand that was not a wand. "Abracadabra, the abacus has now disappeared."

C.C. pulled away the blanket, revealing to no

one's astonishment, having had the trick more than sufficiently ruined for them, that the abacus was indeed no longer there. What was amazing and not expected was that instead of the abacus, there were all eight members of the Pack bunched up together and looking around confused, as if they had just been teleported. This apparently surprised C.C. as well, because she just stood there with her beak hanging open. "I . . . I don't understand how that occurred," she finally said.

"Finally, something C.C. cannot explain," joked Handsome without being mean-spirited, to which everyone laughed.

So despite C.C.'s serious, rational approach, the trick turned out to be magical after all. C.C. left the stage in a daze. "How could it . . . the ratio of probability . . . I can't . . . but . . . what just happened?"

What I will reveal to all of you readers and listeners—what Duane and the others still, to this day, don't know—is that this was all planned earlier along with Sun Girl and the Pack. You see, the thing C.C. *actually* found most scary was not being accepted by everyone she deeply cared for, but she didn't want to tell them that. C.C. figured that sharing a moment of wonder, like she had observed with Handsome and Duane looking at snowflakes through the microscope, would bring her closer. That may seem like a lot of effort and bother to *you*, but I assure you that for C.C., it was a whole lot better than doing more chitchat.

Duane asked for the next performer. "Who would like their turn?"

Major Puff stood up at attention. When he paraded forward, stiffly and proudly, to take his turn on the stage, everyone naturally assumed he would be demonstrating some complicated marching strategy while recounting one of the many battles fought against the great black-backed gulls.

"As a puffin who has descended from a long line of military heroes, my blood has been tempered like that of sharp, cold steel."

A quiet, collective groan was heard in the audience as everyone settled in for what they expected would be a long and tedious affair. But Major Puff's opening speech took a curious turn.

"In keeping with the theme of tonight's entertainment, I shall enflame my blood somewhat and take a leap of faith. I wish to dedicate this performance to Madame," he said while looking nervously at Twitch. He turned and nodded to C.C., who rushed back to one side of the stage and stood beside the object he had first discovered on the Shipwreck—a Victrola. A Victrola is an old-fashioned record player, and if you don't know what a record player is, then I suggest that you ask your parents immediately. Even if you're reading this late at night when you should be sleeping, get up and wake your parents. Tell them it's a story emergency. To continue, C.C. turned the crank of the Victrola with her wing, causing the disc in the middle to turn. Using her beak to serve as the missing needle, C.C. placed the pointy tip onto the rotating record. A scratchy, orchestrated melody spilled out from the horn. Then, to everyone's surprise, Major Puff began to sing.

> When winter's blast approaches
> And frigid air abounds,
> When water freezes over
> And snow doth muffle sound,
> I migrate! I migrate!
> I migrate far from you.

Both Major Puff's voice and his legs quivered during that opening verse, but having gotten through it successfully, his confidence grew.

> When warmer climates beckon
> And palm trees sway hello,
> When jasmine wafts its sweetness
> And white sand warms my toes,
> I migrate! I migrate!
> I migrate far from you.

By the third stanza, Major Puff's voice grew quieter, and dare I say, his blood was stirred with tender passion.

> *When thoughts of you come flooding,*
> *My heart aches in reply.*
> *A North Star there to guide me,*
> *To thee my wings will fly.*
> *I migrate! I migrate!*
> *I migrate home to you.*

Major Puff held the last note on "you" for as long as his breath would allow, bringing everyone to their feet with applause. When he was done, he took a deep, gallant bow as Twitch, who was touched to the core, hopped up to the stage and kissed him softly on the beak. In the annals of puffin history, never did a puffin of such high military rank blush as crimson as the Major.

"Suppose I should have my turn now that I'm up here," said Twitch, turning to the audience. "I'll just nip behind the curtain and get my box of goodies."

Major Puff took his seat, joined by C.C., as the arctic hare dragged out an old wooden chest onto the stage, placing it left of center with the lid opened toward the audience so no one could see what was inside. She stood beside the chest and took a quick, deep breath.

"Bit of a change of pace from the Major's beautiful serenading," Twitch began. "So I've been to the Shipwreck, like a lot of you, checking in with C.C., looking through her books and doing some rummaging, quite a mess in those rooms, could use a little tidying and dusting, maybe some downsizing, just saying."

Twitch's jerks and spasms were now noticeably more intense, which is saying a lot for her. "But here I am, willing and ready, taking the plunge, rolling the dice, trimming the whiskers during a sneezing fit, if you catch my meaning."

No one did take her meaning, but their curiosity was growing nonetheless.

"I learned a new skill, I did. Seemed appropriate for someone like me, the nervous type, always doing several things at once. It's called juggling!"

Twitch leaned over the chest and pulled out a cleaning brush, a feather duster, and a wooden baking spoon. As she continued talking, she began tossing each object into the air, one by one, using her right front foot to throw and the left one to catch, before quickly giving the objects over to the throwing foot again. In this way, she managed to keep the three items aloft in constant motion. "So this is me, busy, busy, busy, always busy, I like to stay busy, helps with the excess energy. I like to cook and bake, as well you know, and I like a clean burrow too, not ashamed of it or proud, just a stickler for such things."

Twitch's newly discovered talent was impressive. She didn't seem to be struggling at all. In fact, she was just warming up. "Can't live a life stuck in a burrow, though, need some fresh air, need some exercise and such. Which is why I make time for my daily cardio-hopping! One hundred, up and down, give or take, just like this!" While still juggling the objects, Twitch began hopping just as she described, never faltering, always stable, causing everyone to break out in spontaneous cheering. But she still wasn't done. "After I met the Major, though, now I could mix things up. The Major taught me marching skills, so there's that, too!" Twitch instantly shifted from hopping up and down to marching back and forth across the stage, with legs high up in the air, while again, still juggling flawlessly.

Major Puff was on his feet. "Bravo, Madame, bravo! Your posture is beyond reproach!"

And then Twitch stopped, catching each of three objects in turn and putting them down. She walked over to center stage, stood beside the chest, and looked out at her friends calmly now. She said, "But juggling is one thing, scary is another. Being the worrying type, most everything to me is scary. Worrying about this, worrying about that, it's in my nature, I suppose. So for the final part of my juggling act, I will push my fears aside, and try to juggle these!" At which point Twitch reached into the chest and pulled out three dangerously sharp–looking knives.

As you probably imagined, a collective gasp was the response to this unexpected program note. It didn't help either that Twitch followed up by saying, "First time trying this bit!" before tossing the knives into the air, one by one. Paws and wings immediately covered the eyes of all who had gathered, but after several seconds had passed lacking any screams of an arctic hare cutting short her juggling career, so to speak, everyone started to relax and watch. Twitch seemed to be the most relaxed. Having found a steady rhythm for keeping the knives in a continual circle of flight, she somehow managed to shift all the juggling responsibilities to one paw, leaving the other one free to reach into the chest.

"Not like me to be having so much fun with all this danger involved," she said with a touch of playful mischief in her voice. "Lots to go wrong, horror and mayhem, sharp blades, softer fur, just saying. Prefer to have a contingency plan, I do, a what-if-things-go-bad, hope-for-the-best-but-expect-the-absolute-worst attitude. Bandages are useful then!" At which moment, Twitch tossed a large roll of bandages into the air along with the juggling knives. "And another, just in case!"

To everyone's delight, Twitch had gone back to

using both paws in order to keep not three but five objects going at once, crisscrossing her throws in front of her, but never allowing either knives or bandages to collide.

"Twitch! Twitch! Twitch!" all her friends shouted, encouraging her on.

"And now for my big finish . . ." Twitch stopped juggling, quickly reached into the chest, grabbed a large iron pot lid, and held it over her head like an umbrella. The sharp knives fell down upon her, only to bounce harmlessly off to the side with a few metallic *dings*. "Ta-da!"

Again, everyone was on their feet applauding, as well as wiping nervous sweat from their brows.

16.
THE BALANCING SHOW CONTINUES, MAGIC IS FORGIVEN, AND THEN SAD NEWS ARRIVES

TWITCH LEFT THE STAGE quite pleased with her-self. Duane was thinking that the Balancing Show was going very well so far. Before he could ask for the next performer, Handsome had already risen to take his turn. *We've had magic, singing, and juggling*, thought Duane. *What amazing talent will Handsome show us, I wonder?* Everyone settled in and gave the musk ox their undivided attention.

"You may not have noticed, but I tend to place a lot of importance on my looks," began Handsome, forcing everyone to smile and politely nod instead of rolling their eyes. "And although I fear many things in this regard—wrinkles, pimples, pustules, liver spots, crow's-feet . . . carbuncles, cold sores, warts, and dryness . . . nose hairs, ear hairs, eye bags, frown lines, to name just a few—it is my fur I am most concerned, and dare I say scared, about."

Handsome turned in profile so everyone could view the length of his body, covered in the long black fur that he spent countless hours brushing and maintaining. "As you can see, my fur is, objectively speaking, truly exquisite. Just the thought of it being damaged in some way can keep me up at night. So I hope all of you can appreciate that for my portion of the evening's entertainment, I have chosen to do this. . . ." At that point Handsome reached up to a piece of cord hanging from the top crossbeam of the stage and pulled it. *Glop!* A bucket full of oozing mud fell over him, leaving his fur looking so much less than exquisite.

Eyes widened as mouths and beaks fell open all at the same time. The silence that accompanied everyone's reaction was deafening. C.C.'s magic trick might have been inexplicable, but Handsome's performance left everyone wondering if they actually saw what they saw. The musk ox just stood there, covered in muck, with an expression of utter revulsion. But witnessing the shocked response he saw from his friends, a small smile appeared that grew and grew until Handsome's body was shaking from belly laughs. "Ho, ho, ho, ho, ho! Ha, ha, ha, ha, ha!" Everyone began to laugh along with him, loudly and boisterously. Even Boo quietly laughed despite herself.

"I only wish I had the foresight to have brought a towelette," Handsome added, causing everyone to break out in another wave of laughter.

After Handsome made his way back to his seat, Duane, Twitch, Sun Girl, and the Pack attempted to clean at least some of the mud off his fur with their paws, feet, and hands. Meanwhile, Magic took to the stage unnoticed. When everyone turned their attention to the front, there she was, standing before them completely motionless. Immediately, the evening's tone shifted from merriment to somber gravity for the very first time. Unspoken, but understood by everyone, was the fact that Magic's turn in the show would determine if life for all of them in the Very, Very Far North would indeed be rebalanced. They were there to bear witness. Boo was there to try to forgive. Magic continued standing silently, her expression a mix of fear and sadness and guilt. The seconds ticked on.

Then, Magic brought one of her front paws up to her nose. Once she withdrew her paw, a bright red nose had replaced her usual black one. With just a tiny sponge filled with red paint concocted by C.C., she changed herself in some inexplicable way. It was still Magic. Everything about her looked like Magic. And yet that dab of red at the end of her face made her somehow a different version of Magic.

Nervous laughter pitter-pattered through the audience like a light rain.

Suddenly, the arctic fox turned around and faced the back of the stage. She spoke, but not in her voice. It was a voice of authority, a parent's voice. "Magic! Your den is a mess! Clean it up right away!" Just as quickly, Magic, with her comical red nose, turned around again. In a higher-pitched, cublike voice she said, "I couldn't possibly, Mother. It's too, too hard!" Magic let her front paws slump forward with exaggerated exhaustion. She turned away again. "Magic, don't give me that nonsense. I said clean your den!" The red-nosed fox began miming that she was cleaning, all the while talking to herself with overdramatic weariness. "It's so tiring. I mean, really! Who would force a little, weak cub like me to work themselves to the bone? It's too much!" Magic threw herself to the ground in a way that was very recognizable to her friends.

"That definitely is Magic," laughed Twitch, to which everyone laughed as well. Duane glanced over to Boo. He could see only the smidgen of a smile, but she was equally engrossed.

Onstage, the voice of authority shifted to a new issue. "Magic! Go and look after your sisters and brothers!" Red-nosed Magic looked out at the audience and groaned. "Ugh! Taking care of them is so boring! I'm bored already! When will it be over? I'm absolutely dying of boredom here!" All the while, she showed herself struggling to overcome her lack of interest, shaking her head quickly, slapping her cheeks to wake up, jumping up and down, but to no avail. She fell to the ground, rolled on her back, and groaned pathetically. "Ohh, ohh, ohh!"

Everyone couldn't help but laugh loudly now. Here was an over-the-top version of their over-the-top friend. They might have considered it rude to be laughing at her behind her back but for the fact that the only difference between the actual Magic and the one onstage was a splotch of red paint.

In the snap of a finger, she was up again, going back and forth between her parent voice and her younger voice.

"Magic! Did you glue leaves on your brothers and sisters?"

"Just on their front paws so they would have wings to fly away."

"Magic! Your brothers and sisters are crying and won't go to sleep!"

"They wanted a story before bed. I didn't know they wouldn't like ghost stories."

"Magic! You left your brothers and sisters alone on the mountain!"

"We were playing hide-and-seek!"

"Magic," said the strict voice, less angry but more serious, "they could have been hurt because of your lack of concern."

Magic stopped. The laughter stopped. This was

the moment she was leading to, the part that was most scary to her. She had shown everyone that since the day she lied to them and hurt Boo, she had been looking at herself and reflecting on what she saw. She had painted a comical portrait of the impulsive, self-centered version of Magic, which was part of who she was, but not all. She showed them that she could see there were consequences to her choices, and they weren't always good. Now she reached up and wiped the red paint off. She looked out at her audience, and then up toward the back, where Boo stood watching her. "I promise to try to be a better friend."

Boo held Magic's gaze for a moment, and then she nodded ever so slightly.

There was a collective sigh of relief, as the expression goes. Magic came down from the stage to hugs and smiles. Boo came in closer to the group. No one was happier than Duane, though. The Balancing Show had done what it was supposed to do, and he felt at peace. And then, on the far side of the celebration, Duane spotted the weasel. Of course he was there—he was everywhere. But by his expression, it was clear that he was not happy with how things turned out. When he discovered that Duane was staring at him, he sneered back before scurrying away in a snit.

"Duane, you haven't had your turn yet," said Magic.

"Hmm? Sorry?" he asked.

"Yes, that's right, he hasn't. Take your seats, everybody," Twitch announced. "Duane is up next."

Duane didn't have anything nearly as spectacular as what his friends had shown. His bit was really quite short and self-contained. "I tried to think of something that would be really scary for me," he said once he got onstage, "and this is what I came up with." Duane closed his eyes. He was going to concentrate on a single thought. It was the thought he feared the most in the world, to the point that he would rather avoid imagining it. But he wouldn't this time. He would hold steady and—

"What? For me? Oh, I see."

It was Handsome's voice Duane heard with his eyes still closed. When he opened them, he caught a glimpse of another musk ox just leaving. Meanwhile, Handsome was holding a letter that he now was in the middle of reading. His expression was grave. "Oh my," he said softly.

"What is it?" asked C.C.

Handsome put the letter down. "My older brother has injured himself. He is the leader of the herd, you understand. I've been asked home to take over for him. Tomorrow, I . . . I will have to leave."

Duane remained standing onstage alone. Naturally, the shocking news took attention away from his performance. Everyone gathered around Handsome to suss out the details of his family situation, what happened to his brother, how to lead a herd, and so on.

Not Duane, though. He was very quiet. What no one knew was that the thought Duane was going to force himself to imagine, the thing that he found most scary and that he would rather avoid more than anything else in the world, was in fact the thing that actually just happened. Duane was about to lose one of his friends.

17.
ONE QUESTION

Duane could never predict upon waking up how he would greet the morning, or indeed, how the morning would greet him. It was best when they received each other cheerfully, but this wasn't always the case.

Sometimes the morning greeted Duane by dumping so much snow in front of his cave that he could not see a thing. When that happened, Duane understood that the morning was not in a good mood and would prefer to be left alone.

Respectfully, Duane would crawl back into bed and sleep until the afternoon came along.

Sometimes the morning stayed so silent and still that Duane could barely tell if it *had* arrived. On those occasions, he, too, would stay as quiet as he could. He'd tiptoe outside with a big, comforting mug of ice tea and sit on the Fabulous Beach. Then, by keeping his breath muted, his heart calm, and his tea-slurping to a minimum, Duane let the morning know that he was listening should there be anything it wanted to share.

Sometimes the morning was all business, rush, rush, rush, ushering into the cave Duane's friends with demands or reminders, filling the early hours with shouts and scolds or frets and sniffles. Busy mornings, just like grumpy mornings, were ideally handled by staying in bed with the covers pulled tightly over his head.

But there were also times when the morning was altogether jolly and Duane wasn't. Those were usually the mornings that arrived after difficult nights, sometimes with tummy aches or with bad dreams. They didn't happen often, but they happened.

Such was the case on the morning after learning that Handsome would be leaving the Very, Very Far North, perhaps for good. In fact, Handsome was going to leave later that day because the letter insisted he come and lead the musk ox herd as soon as possible. Twitch organized a send-off for Handsome in his field for the afternoon, a happy farewell to mark his passage and a chance for everyone to express their love. That was the plan, anyway.

Duane sat up at the edge of his mattress, not sleepy, not energetic, not anything, really. He yawned and stretched, but his heart wasn't into it. He considered having a big, distracting breakfast, but his stomach wasn't into it. Meanwhile, outside, the morning happily awaited Duane's appearance, spreading rays of sunshine in front of his cave entrance like a welcome mat. Duane groaned in resignation, then stumbled to his feet and lumbered out of his cave.

In all the many ways Duane had left his home in the past, he had no name for the way he was doing it that morning. It wasn't an adventure hike. It wasn't a thinking walk. It wasn't a social call or an emergency run or a stroll down memory lane. Instinctually, Duane headed left, thus avoiding having to pass by Handsome's field. He hadn't spoken to his friend since the night before, at the Balancing Show. Handsome shared his letter with everyone while Duane was on the stage imagining what it would be like to lose one of his friends. Duane did not join the group that had gathered around Handsome. He didn't express his shock or sadness, nor did he heartily endorse Twitch's send-off idea; he couldn't find the words inside him. Instead, Duane walked off the stage, past everyone, and headed up to his cave. "Duane!" shouted Handsome after him. "Duane, don't you want to hear . . . ?"

He had so many feelings, too many feelings—a tangled mess.

Now Duane walked and walked, without a plan

or destination, until he reached the flatlands. Nothing interesting ever happened here, unless the unexpected happened, but he'd had enough of the unexpected, thank you very much. On the flatlands, there was nothing to look at, nor was there anything new to grow curious about. Duane kicked a rock. He lowered his head so that he stared only at the ground and charged forward. He would go on like that forever, he decided.

The morning stayed with him, sunny as ever, but eventually it felt a little snubbed. It gave up on the polar bear, took the sun, and carried it up toward noontime. Duane didn't notice. It would take a familiar voice to get his attention.

"Hello, Duane."

Duane looked up. There stood Sun Girl and the Pack. He had walked right past them.

"Hi," Duane replied, but not in his usual happy way.

"Your head was down. Are you searching for something?"

Sun Girl's question caught Duane by surprise. *Searching for something?* he asked himself. *Is that what I'm doing?* Then Duane's eyes got watery. "I don't know," he finally said out loud. "I feel sad, and I can't make myself feel not sad."

Sun Girl nodded in understanding. "Maybe it's a day to see the Walrus."

Of all the suggestions Duane might have considered offering to someone if they were in a similar situation, seeing a walrus would not have made his top five, or top twenty-five, for that matter. He'd never met a walrus, although he'd seen a picture in one of C.C.'s books. In any case, Sun Girl said he should see *the* Walrus, not *a* walrus.

"Who is the Walrus?" asked Duane.

"'*What* is the Walrus?' might be a better question. Let me tell you a story." Sun Girl went up to the confused polar bear and took his enormous paw in her hand and walked with him and told him the story and then explained what he should do. The Pack followed behind at a respectful distance, out of earshot, and as your narrator, so shall I in relating this private moment. Even narrators have to know their proper place from time to time.

When Sun Girl finished explaining, Duane agreed that a visit to the Walrus might be just what he needed. "Which way do I go?" he asked.

The Pack made a large circle around him. Then they all turned outward and pointed. "It's your choice," said Sun Girl. "Pick a direction."

"Any direction?" Duane asked.

Sun Girl nodded. "That's how it works."

Duane closed his eyes and turned around several times, but not enough to make himself dizzy. When he opened his eyes, he began walking as Sun Girl and the Pack waved and wished him good luck. This time, Duane did not look down. He looked toward the horizon. He wasn't on an adventure hike, nor was he on a thinking walk. This time he was on both, combined, just as Sun Girl had instructed.

Had Duane looked up, he would have spotted

Major Puff circling the sky above his location just then. Suddenly, the puffin broke off from his flying pattern and headed directly to Duane, where he landed beside him.

"There you are," the Major said with great relief. "I've been searching high and low."

"Hello, Major Puff," said Duane, who continued walking forward with determination, which forced the puffin to march along with him to keep up.

"Madame had asked me to remind everyone of the party for Handsome this afternoon to make sure they come," replied the puffin. "Now that I've found you, my mission has been completed successfully, and I can return to my marching practice back at the burrow."

But before Major Puff could take off, Duane said, "I did remember the party, but I can't go until I find the Walrus."

Major Puff's mission just got complicated.

"But . . . but Madame said I need to . . . to make

sure that . . . um, the Walrus, you say? Who is this walrus?"

"I don't know," said Duane. "It may not even *be* a walrus."

"Oh? Oh . . . um, but you definitely must find it?"

"Yes, in order to ask a question."

"And what question would that be?"

"I don't know yet," replied Duane. "But that's what Sun Girl instructed. She said I would know the question when I met the Walrus, and it would help me be less sad."

Major Puff could not make heads or tails of Duane's explanation. It did not fit in the reasoned calculations that a military puffin such as himself would use in decision-making. But Duane did mention being sad, and the Major certainly understood that. It was an emotion he had often felt before he met Twitch. *Best keep an eye on the lad*, he thought to himself, *until we establish who this walrus is*. He continued walking alongside his friend.

Duane appreciated the company. Even if he

wasn't really in the mood to talk, he felt less isolated. So the polar bear and the puffin continued together toward an unknown destination. As far as their direction, though, they soon reached the Cold, Cold Ocean. Duane supposed he could continue straight in and swim, but it didn't feel right, now that Major Puff was at his side. And Sun Girl never said he couldn't change direction while in search of the Walrus, so he did. The two friends turned and followed the shoreline. They did not travel far before they were joined by Magic and Boo.

"There you are, Duane!" shouted Magic, using overly dramatic paw gestures. "Ever since Major Puff said you weren't in your cave, we've been looking everywhere! We've probably searched the Very, Very Far North at least five times already! I mean, really!"

"Actually, we came directly here when we saw Major Puff swoop down from the sky," Boo said.

Duane didn't hear Boo, but he did take note of the fact that she and Magic were together. He continued walking forward, along with marching Major

Puff, forcing Magic and Boo to keep up with him if they wanted answers, which Magic certainly did.

"Why are you here in the middle of nowhere, Duane?" demanded Magic. "There is a party to prepare for, after all! There will likely be nibbles!"

Before Duane could answer, Major Puff stepped in. He realized that the mission had changed, and as a Puff, he should take a leadership role. "Duane will not attend the party until the Walrus has been dealt with."

"A walrus?" Magic asked, scrunching up her nose in bewilderment. "Why does he need to deal with a walrus?"

"Not *a* walrus," corrected Major Puff with severe conviction, "but *the* Walrus."

Magic was losing patience. "Where is this walrus?" she insisted. "Who is it and why is it so important? I mean, really!"

"He doesn't know where exactly, or who exactly, but when they meet, Duane will ask the Walrus a question yet unknown so he won't feel sad."

Even for an arctic fox who liked to play tricks, this was strange territory. Magic and Boo shared a confused look, but then they shrugged. Strange or not, they both knew about feeling sad of late, so if this "wild-walrus chase" would make Duane feel not sad, they were on board.

Duane was now accompanied by three friends, side by side. He walked as Major Puff marched while Boo pranced and Magic jumped and skipped. He definitely didn't feel alone in his sadness, which was comforting, but only up to a point. His thoughts kept returning to Handsome. He was such a good friend, and Duane couldn't imagine him out of his life. He couldn't imagine what tomorrow would feel like. Would Handsome's absence be unbearable? Would there be a hole left that couldn't be filled?

As if his companions could read Duane's mind or sense his mood, the topic of conversation turned to the musk ox. "The first time I met Handsome, I believed him to be a great black-backed gull, my mortal enemy," said Major Puff. "I even challenged him to a duel in the middle of the river! Ho-ho, I daresay he was not pleased." The Major recounted the memory with such good humor, Duane couldn't help but smile too.

"And Duane, remember when you took me to Handsome's afternoon tea and I was blue and *without* an invitation?" Magic said.

"You attended one of Handsome's events without an invitation?" Major Puff gasped. "He must have been livid!"

Duane did not join in the talk, but silently, he remembered the day clearly. *We didn't know what to do with her! She kept grabbing food from our plates and pouring her own tea and talking, talking, talking the whole time. Handsome should have been very upset. He worked so hard to make everything perfect, but he didn't say a word in complaint. In fact, once he realized there was no stopping Magic being Magic, he just relaxed and enjoyed the craziness.*

Duane laughed out loud. His companions stopped talking and took notice. Duane took notice as well. It was the lightest he had felt all day.

The quartet continued on, still without any idea of where or what they were doing, but with a sense of purpose that seemed both serious and silly. Would they find the Walrus? Duane could not know for sure, but it was a quest his friends pledged their loyalty to and were committed to seeing through.

And then C.C. arrived. She landed in front of them with her wings stretched out. They all were forced to stop.

"I am here to inform you that according to Twitch, the party has been moved to the Fabulous Beach, which is straight ahead, for those of you who are geographically challenged."

Major Puff stepped forward and declared in a most official voice, "We cannot attend this party until Duane has met with the Walrus." Then he awaited all the follow-up questions that he expected C.C. to ask. The snowy owl didn't satisfy that expectation.

"Yes, I know," replied C.C.

"Oh? . . . Um, not *a* walrus, mind you, but *the* Walrus!"

"Yes, I know," C.C. repeated. "Who may or may not be an *actual* walrus."

"Aha! But what you don't realize is that we don't know where the Walrus is," Major Puff countered triumphantly. "We haven't a clue. This is a completely oblivious effort."

"Yes, I know," said C.C. simply. "Nor does Duane know the question he will ask if he finds the Walrus."

Everyone stared at C.C. with their mouths wide open. Then Magic grew annoyed and threw herself to the ground dramatically. "Is there anything you don't know, C.C.? I mean, really!"

"Probably," replied C.C. after a moment's consideration. "But regarding all this Walrus information, Sun Girl told me as we were setting up the party."

"Oh," said Duane, deflated. That may have explained C.C.'s inside knowledge, but it still left him confused. It seemed that Sun Girl knew where he was heading. *Was the search just a fool's errand?*

Duane wondered. *Was there no Walrus after all?*

"What should we do, Duane?" asked Magic gently.

The sadness that Duane awoke with was not the same sadness he felt now. It wasn't mixed with anger for Handsome abandoning him or despair that he'd be all alone. Duane's other friends were around him now, supporting him, worrying about him, making him smile, wanting only the best. It gave him courage. It allowed him to feel only the sadness of Handsome leaving but still with lots of room for the love he had for Handsome too.

As for the Walrus, Duane wouldn't give up on their meeting just yet because not everything was settled within the polar bear's heart. Not knowing who or what the Walrus was meant that he just needed to stay alert in case the Walrus should suddenly show up. In the meantime, Duane was ready to take a different leap of faith.

"Let's go to the Fabulous Beach and say goodbye to our friend."

* * *

At the Fabulous Beach, Duane and his companions found a large blanket already laid out, and in the center was a mound of nibbles. It was to be a picnic party, which in its simplicity was always their favorite kind. When Handsome made his way down from his field, past the berry bushes and onto the shoreline, everyone gave him a big "Hurrah!"

"You are all too kind," said Handsome, truly moved.

The party itself was a whirlwind of activity, and I'm afraid I got too swept up in it myself to give you a proper account. There was plenty of laughter, and the retelling of stories, and gentle teasing. At one point, the Pack regaled Handsome with a choral piece created just for him, entitled "Noble Handsome, King of the Musk Oxen." At the end of the song, Sun Girl crowned him with a garland of wildflowers that he wore unabashedly for the rest of the celebration. And yes, there were quiet moments too that came unexpectedly, pauses in the conversation that were filled with the shared somber understanding of why they were all there. In those moments, a tear was shed, followed by a pat on the back, but then a joke was made and then another, until joy reigned supreme again.

When it was time for Handsome to leave, the friends gave their goodbyes one by one. Duane held back, watching, hesitant, a bit nervous. *How do you properly say goodbye to someone so important in your life?* And then Duane had a thought. Maybe he *did* find the Walrus, because as Sun Girl had explained, the Walrus can be different things depending on who is seeking it and what they need to know. In Duane's case, the Walrus turned out to be a musk ox. When his turn came to say goodbye, he knew just what to say.

"Handsome, you won't forget me, will you?" *That* was the question Duane had to ask, and he needed to know its answer. "You won't forget me, right? Because I certainly won't ever forget you."

Handsome looked at Duane and replied, "No, never. I promise."

Duane nodded. Then he moved to one side and allowed Handsome to walk past and go where life was taking him, far and away.

That night Duane lay on his mattress staring up at the roof of his cave. Moonlight filled his cozy home with a silvery glow. The armless grandfather clock in the corner tick-talked away about the future and the possibilities it held. But Duane was not listening. He'd listen another time, but not that night. That night was for remembering.

18.
THE NEXT DAY AND THEN SOME

IN THE MORNING OF the day after Handsome had left, Duane awoke to singing. He quickly determined it wasn't him singing and it most certainly wouldn't have been the weasel. The melody being sung was light and breezy, it came from outside, and the voice lifting it was joyful and pure. Duane did not recognize the music or the singer. He felt compelled to find its source. So, forgoing any breakfast, he left his cave and followed where his curiosity—and his ears—led.

His search did not require traveling far. Having strolled down the path from his cave, he arrived at what used to be Handsome's field. It should have been empty, but it was not. One of Duane's other friends was there, going about the space, tidying and grooming, stopping for bits of grazing, interspersed with snippets of song.

"Hello, Boo," said Duane softly.

The caribou did not flinch in fright. She did not instinctually position herself ready to escape at a split-second moment. Boo only turned her face toward Duane and offered him a big, open smile. It was a smile of understanding and tenderness, whose warmth found its way across the field and reached the polar bear's poor, bruised heart.

Duane said, "Boo, your voice was so love—"

Boo leaped up, not startled, but she meant to cut Duane off. He didn't understand.

"I just wanted to say that—"

Boo leaped again, this time following it with a semi-serious expression of reproach.

Duane semi-understood. "You mean I'm not supposed to—"

Boo cut him off with another disapproving look. And before Duane could say a further word, Boo tilted her head to the side, to direct his attention to a chair at one end of the reflective pond. Boo nudged her head toward it, encouraging Duane to sit. This time Duane completely understood and obeyed. He walked over to the chair and sat.

On the far side of the pond, Boo stood facing him, still and relaxed. She took a slow, deep breath, and then softly and delicately, Boo positioned herself into a pose. She raised a front hoof and held it out before her as if she were cradling something, and by the expression on her face, by her concentration as she looked at it, it was made clear to Duane that this something was very precious.

Then Boo began to dance.

I will remind you readers and listeners that Duane had not had the privilege of seeing Boo dance priorly, having not been part of the group that spied on her. But what the others witnessed was a private dance that Boo did for herself. It was not meant to be seen. The dance that Duane was now watching was quite the opposite. It was a gift given to him from Boo. It was a dance that told the story of friendship.

As she spun and rolled and twisted, as she stretched and vaulted and soared, as she collapsed and swelled and caved and blossomed, the invisible, precious something that Boo created in front of Duane at the start always stayed close to her, protected. Boo passed it from one hoof to the other; she balanced it on the curve of her back or between the forks of her antlers. Duane saw it throughout the dance. He never took his eyes off the invisible, precious something. His heart was invested in its safety. *How is that possible?* he wondered. Dancing was a whole new language for Duane. He didn't think he should be able to understand it, and yet he did. Through Boo's perfect and precise movements, through the energy that flowed in and out of her body, through her strength and speed and lightness, he began to read the wordless story she was telling him. And Duane understood too that he was in this tale, and it delighted him. He stared and smiled as Boo became him, in his happy, lumbering walk, in his kind and gentle expression. Boo became Handsome, in his stillness and his frowns, in his self-importance and in his sense of honor. At times the dance was comical, provoking Duane to laugh in recognition. At other times, the dance was poignant in expressing all that can never be properly said in just words about friendship, about the wide chasm of difference and misunderstanding between souls, and about what a miracle it is when two can manage to span such distance. At the conclusion of Boo's performance, when the tale was all but told and the kaleidoscope of feelings were given each their due, Boo returned her focus to the invisible, imaginary yet precious something that she delicately held throughout her dance. She lifted it into the air, and finally set it free. Duane followed Boo's gaze skyward, and together they watched it go.

Duane sighed. This was what he had needed. Boo

did what the Balancing Show was supposed to do before it was thrown out of balance by Handsome's departure. She made everything okay again, at least for Duane.

And so Boo moved in to the field previously occupied by Handsome. It wasn't something she needed to do, as the place she had was more than adequate for her privacy needs. I suppose she may have done it for Duane's sake, to help fill the void left by his absent friend. Or she may have done it for her own sake, to not be quite so isolated and to take the risk of feeling foolish or embarrassed now and then, but

also to take the risk of being accepted as well. And who's to say that perhaps she didn't do it for both their sakes, because isn't that also possible?

For Duane, the arrangement was wonderful. Boo wasn't a replacement for Handsome, because no true friend can be replaced by another. For Duane, it was the beginning of a new friendship, one that had not really been explored yet, that had a different shape and rhythm than all his other friendships. Boo and Duane did not speak much. When they shared each other's company, it was often done silently. Questions were posed with small gestures: a lifted bowl, for example—*would you like to join me for some breakfast berries?* Replies were given the same way: a small smile and slow blink—*thank you, I'd like that.* Conversation was equally sparse, a deep, content breath—*summer is coming.* A rotation of an ear and a playful raise of a brow—*Magic is coming.*

As for the weasel, he remained among Duane and his friends, but he was ignored for the most part. Duane didn't go to the effort of naming him. He didn't feel it would serve any purpose to bring the weasel into focus in that way. Left alone, the weasel wasn't too much of a bother. After all, he was only interested in crumbs, whether it was food or friendship. Should the weasel ever come to a decision that crumbs were no longer enough, Duane would be most happy to invite him to his table for a proper meal.

Many months later, a letter arrived. Duane found it on the ground at the entrance of his cave. How it got there or who delivered it, I cannot say. But who the letter was from was made clear as soon as Duane picked it up.

To: Duane & Company
From: Handsome the musk ox, Esquire

The words were written on the envelope with the same flourished handwriting that defined all of his correspondence, whether it be invitations for afternoon tea

or letters of complaint to the narrator for unflattering descriptions of musk oxen.

Duane did not open it right away. His reading skills had improved considerably under C.C.'s tutelage, so he understood from the envelope that the letter was meant for everyone. He made the rounds and announced the news. Soon everyone was gathered at his cave, waiting for Duane to start in.

Dear Duane,

I trust that you have assembled all our friends for the reading of my letter. If you haven't, then do so at once. A letter begins to lose its oomph by the third or fourth retelling. I do not wish my eloquent sentiments and observations to be recited in a tired, bored voice.

As of writing this, I am hard at work leading my herd. It is tedious business, I assure you. Deciding upon where to graze or dine for a large group is maddening. One musk ox might have allergies, another is simply picky, and the bickering is never-ending. Eventually one simply must put their hoof down and say enough is enough.

As for the general quality of grooming among the members, I can summarize it in just one word: appalling. My brother has allowed standards to plummet. It's as if they've never heard of a nose-hair trimmer before. I've initiated several countermeasures, including a mandatory lecture series cleverly entitled A Brushup on Brushes, as well as a drop-in clinic for one-on-one consultations. Attendance, so far, has been sparse.

On a different note, it is said that absence makes the heart grow fonder. I confess that I must agree with the sentiment. There is not a night that goes by that I do not think of all of you, heave a heavy sigh, but wish only the best. If I could have but . . .

Apologies. My letter-writing was just interrupted by my brother. I suddenly have good news to share. I will be returning after all, in several months' time. My brother informs me that he is recovering much more quickly than anticipated and will soon resume his rightful position. He looks in terrible shape, if you ask me, but when I pointed that out, he also added that the herd

finds me somewhat annoying. I don't know what my small-minded relatives have to grumble about, but if that's their verdict, then I shall not complain.

So there you have it. I shall be once again in the Very, Very Far North! But I must warn you that leadership may have changed me. Upon my return, you might encounter a musk ox less casual and carefree than the one who left.

Your dear, dear friend, always,
Handsome the musk ox, Esquire

ACKNOWLEDGMENTS

My journey to the Very, Very Far North would not be possible without the navigation skills of three important people. I wish to thank my editor, Reka Simonsen; my agent, Hilary McMahon; and my always-first reader, Dominique.